Books by Larry Callen

Pinch
The Deadly Mandrake
Sorrow's Song

Sorrow's Song

WHOOPER

Larry Callen

Sorrow's Song

ILLUSTRATED BY MARVIN FRIEDMAN

An Atlantic Monthly Press Book
BOSTON   Little, Brown and Company   TORONTO

FIRST EDITION

"Life Gets Tee-Jus, Don't It" (p. 35). Words and Music by Carson J. Robison. © Copyright 1948 by MCA MUSIC, A Division of MCA Inc., New York, New York. Copyright renewed. Used by permission. All rights reserved.

"You Are My Sunshine" by Jimmie Davis and Charles Mitchell. Copyright 1941 by Peer International Corporation. Copyright Renewed. Used by permission.

Library of Congress Cataloging in Publication Data

Callen, Larry.
  Sorrow's song.

  "An Atlantic Monthly Press book."
  SUMMARY: Sorrow Nix, a young girl who can't talk, befriends an injured whooping crane and in protecting it comes to better understand freedom and friendship.
  [1. Mutism—Fiction. 2. Physically handicapped—Fiction.
3. Whooping cranes—Fiction]
I. Friedman, Marvin. II. Title.
PZ7.C135So   [Fic]   78-31789
ISBN 0-316-12497-4

ATLANTIC–LITTLE, BROWN BOOKS
ARE PUBLISHED BY
LITTLE, BROWN AND COMPANY
IN ASSOCIATION WITH
THE ATLANTIC MONTHLY PRESS

Published simultaneously in Canada
by Little, Brown & Company (Canada) Limited

PRINTED IN THE UNITED STATES OF AMERICA

To a bunch of Callens
Willa, Erin, Alex, Dashiel, Holly,
Emily, Lawrence, Dorothy, David, Ann, and Toni

To some very special in-laws
Alphonse Adam Autin
Mary Waguespack Callen
Sophia Lee Carmouche
Ernest Massicot Carmouche
Lorraine Whitman Carmouche
Hollis Robert Carmouche
William Jeter Carmouche, Jr.
Dianna Carmouche Engolio
Guy Joseph Engolio
Gay Carmouche Grimball
Lester James Grimball
Miles Donald Ledbetter
Andree Carmouche Stansbury
Michael Kenneth Stansbury
Mimi Carmouche Talkington
Alan Lee Talkington
Eugene Templeton Woods II

And to the sons and daughters
of Whooper and her friend

Contents

Sorrow's Song

1

The Zoo Man

THE ZOO MAN came riding into Four Corners on a coal black wagon pulled by a coal black mule. I never saw a farm wagon painted black before. It was moving slow, creaking and rolling side to side. It crept closer. I couldn't have stopped looking at it if I wanted to. I took Sorrow Nix's hand and jerked her to the side of the road.

The wagon stopped right in front of us. A big, bushy-haired man sat in the driver's seat, skinny nosed and frowning. His eyes were on me. He didn't say a word.

Sorrow touched my arm and my eyes went first to her and then quickly to the back of the wagon. Near the tailgate, a red hound and a little red pup were sitting on their haunches, staring at us with huge brown eyes.

"You got a pet possum?" a voice asked sharply.

I looked at the Zoo Man.

"No."

"Got any kind of pets at all?"

"I got a pig."

"Ain't interested in pigs. Any kids around here got a bobcat for a pet?"

"No."

He nodded. Then he gave the reins a flick and moved off. He didn't look back one single time.

We followed behind the noisy wagon with the two dogs keeping their eyes on us. When we got to the IC railroad pasture where there is a break in the barbed wire fence, the Zoo Man drove his mule through the shallow ditch and into the cow pasture. He pulled way back off the road before he drew in on the reins. Then he climbed down one slow step at a time, unhitched his black mule and let it roam. He checked the two cages in the front part of the wagon. Inside one was a white turkey with only one eye. Inside the other was a brown fox who had seen better days. He took a big canvas sign off his black wagon, walked back to the road where we were watching, and hammered it into the ground with a hand ax. When we moved closer to read the sign, he furled his bushy eyebrows and took a step toward us.

"I'm looking to buy animals for the city zoo," he said. "Any kind of animals at all. You go home and tell your friends." He raised the hand ax over his head and crashed it down on top of one of the IC railroad's fence posts. You could hear the post split a mile.

Sorrow and I backed away from him. I've got a fair share of respect for axes in the hands of strangers.

He stood next to his sign like the two of them were guarding the break in the fence. I looked at the sign for the first time.

GENUINE ZOO ANIMALS.
I PAY GOOD.

"Don't this town have no animals at all?" he yelled. But he wasn't really looking for an answer. His mind was on getting his sign up.

Everything he said sounded like he was yelling. But he didn't really scare us too much, even though he was trying hard. You can tell about grown-ups if you study them. Some of them yell pretty good, but if you wait out their yelling, they will sooner or later start saying please do this or please do that. Then you can decide whether you want to do it or not. Other kinds don't say a word. They just look at you, and you know if you don't do what they are thinking, there's going to be a problem. My dad's pretty much like that. But the Zoo Man was somewhere in between. You could tell he wasn't really a mean man. Mean men are the worst kind. My dad says they are like a wagon with a cracked wheel. If they don't get fixed, they are going to do somebody harm sooner or later.

"What you kids doing out of school?"

"We are on our way," I told him.

He looked at Sorrow. She was smiling at the red puppy.

"Is he telling the truth, pretty girl?" he asked.

Sorrow Nix is as good a friend as I ever hope to have. She is so smart, I don't even like to think about it. She knows words I never heard of.

But Sorrow can't use words the way most people can. Sorrow can't talk. I don't know why she can't talk. That's just the way it's always been.

She looked at him. It was always hardest when she

tried to talk to someone for the first time. She smiled. She nodded her head. But he kept looking at her, waiting for her to say something to him. Finally she got tired of being stared at and pulled a piece of paper out of her pocket. She searched around for a pencil and started writing.

"We are on our way," she wrote.

"What's the matter with you?" he asked. "Cat got your tongue?" He was smiling. Sorrow looked up at him and smiled back. Didn't bother her any that he didn't know she couldn't talk.

"Gimme your hand," he said. She did, not knowing what was on his mind. He started squeezing it hard in his big hand. Sorrow looked up at him. If she could have cried out, she would have. Instead she only moaned and tried to pull her hand back. There were tears welling in her eyes.

The Zoo Man dropped her hand. His big arms plopped to his sides. He looked at her and pulled his fingers to his face like he was praying. I could hear him breathe into his hands.

"Can't you really talk?" He looked at her. "Lord, child, I'm truly sorry. I never would've squeezed your soft, little hand so hard 'less I thought you were trying to make fun of me." He looked at Sorrow. Now it was his turn to have watery eyes.

He opened up his arms and moved closer to her. He wanted to give her a hug. But she backed off. She wasn't too keen on being hugged by strangers who went around squeezing girls' hands. When he saw that she wasn't going to let him hug her, he stopped.

"What's your name?" he asked.

At first she didn't do a thing. Then she slowly pulled out her crumpled brown piece of paper and her pencil and wrote her name.

"Sorrow's no name for a little girl," he said. He looked at her for the longest time. Then his eyes dropped to the ground like he was thinking of something. Something sad. All of a sudden his head popped up and he stared her straight in the eyes.

"I never knew a person who couldn't talk in my whole life. You seen a doctor about it?"

It was kind of funny. Not to him, but to us. Sorrow knew she couldn't talk. Maybe she would like to, but it didn't bother her too much. She never told me it did.

2

The Three-legged Toad

THE ZOO MAN said he would be coming back to Four Corners again even though he hadn't gotten any animals the first visit. I was thinking long and hard about that on a cold winter morning when I met Mr. John Barrow strutting down the road carrying a burlap sack on his shoulder. He is kind of a friend of mine, but he is a sly one and you got to watch him close.

"You know what I got in this here sack, Pinch?" he asked. He was scratching his skinny self, like always, and jiggling the sack. "It's a genuine three-legged frog I jist caught on the edge of the swamp. It's the biggest one I ever saw. And you don't often catch a frog when the weather is cold. When the Zoo Man gits back, he's going to pay me plenty money for this frog."

I never had a three-legged frog before. I never even saw a three-legged frog. I asked him if he wanted to sell it and he said that would be all right with him, except the price of a genuine three-legged frog would have to be higher than the regular frog price, 'cause there couldn't be too many three-legged frogs and that made them worth a lot of money. I hadn't heard that before, but it made some sense. 'Course, I had doubts that a frog with only three legs would bring more money at the Farmers' Market than I got for the four-legged kind. But it might be fun just owning a three-legged frog.

He pulled it out of the sack and dangled it up for me to see. One look was enough to show what kind of an ornery man I was dealing with, 'cause it wasn't even a three-legged frog. It was a three-legged toad.

"Mr. John Barrow, that's a warty old toad. I don't know anybody who has a taste for fried toad legs. Even a dog can get sick from eating a toad."

He jiggled the toad by one leg.

"I'm surprised at you. This surely ain't an eating frog. It's a collecting frog."

"It's a toad," I told him.

"Why, even if you are right, did you ever see a three-legged toad before? I imagine there'd be hundreds of people willing to pay a whole pile of dollars jist to have this cute little fellow as a pet. How you suppose he lasted as long as he did with only three legs?"

He was holding the toad up close to his face to get a good look, and the old toad didn't look any too comfortable. I'd have felt the same way if I was it.

"Pinch, jist how you think he lost his leg? It must've been a ferocious battle, maybe even with an alligator. He's a fat and spunky feller. You got to see that, jist by looking at him."

The old toad had one of its front legs missing. There was hardly a stump. Its back legs were still in good shape for hopping. For a fact, it was a cute looking little toad, warts and all. I didn't know anybody who had a three-legged toad for a pet. I didn't even know anybody who wanted one. But somebody might.

"The toad sure is a skinny one, don't you think?"

I was trying out a bargaining trick I learned right from Mr. John Barrow. Skinny toads sell cheaper than fat ones.

"Well, son, the trouble is your specialty is frogs. You got to be a real toad man to know what a valuable thing this particular toad really is."

He put the toad back in the sack. Then he sat on a tree stump and squiggled around to get comfortable. His two skinny legs were stretched out about a mile in front of him. He started holding real still 'cause there was a mosquito hawk flitting around his shoe and he wanted to see if it would light.

"Why, Pinch —" he spoke softly, watching the little insect flit around "— that toad's got more health than he has a right to. You seen toads sitting there and not moving a muscle. That takes a lot of self-control to do. You know that, Pinch. Why, look how hard it is to jist hold a fishing pole still long enough to git a nibble. That's about the hardest thing there is to do, sitting still like that. And the old toad does it practically all day long." The mosquito hawk moved away, but Mr. John Barrow didn't move a single muscle, 'cause now he was imitating the toad.

"I'll give you a nickel for him, just as he is," I told him.

Right then Charley Riedlinger came running up. He took one look at the toad and asked Mr. John Barrow, "What you got there?" And Mr. John Barrow said he had a very valuable animal that he had developed a true affection for, and he kept talking like that, watching Charley with a cocked eye to see if he was getting interested.

I wasn't being taken in by his fancy sales talk, but the toad *might* be worth more than a nickel and I just might find a use for it. I might even sell it to the schoolteacher for about thirty cents so she could use it to teach about animals and things. I broke in on his sales talk and told him: "Mr. John Barrow, I'll give you a dime for that poor toad."

But by then he had hooked Charley so hard that Charley offered him fifteen cents right then and there. That ended it, 'cause I didn't have fifteen cents to spend on a toad.

3

The Gift

I STOPPED AT Sorrow's house like I usually do every morning and the two of us walked to school. I told her about the bargaining, but I shouldn't have done it, 'cause it just set her to thinking about that poor crippled toad. She didn't smile one time the rest of the way to school.

We got seated just before the bell rang, and about two minutes later Charley Riedlinger dashed in with a big smile on his face. It was almost like he was happy at being late. I sat there, waiting for the schoolteacher to stomp all over him.

Charley stuck his hand inside his shirt and pulled out the toad. Then he *gave* it to the schoolteacher, even though he'd spent his fifteen cents on that silly toad. Why, he was sweet on her is what it was, even if she was way over twenty and old enough to be his mother.

He stood there holding it out to her. I wouldn't have figured it to happen, but after she got used to the idea she reached out and took the toad just like it was the natural thing for her to do. What happened next turned my stomach, 'cause she stood up there and told the whole class what a nice thing Charley had done. She said how sweet he was to do it and that the toad was one of the finest gifts she ever got.

The toad just sat there in the box near the window all morning long, with everybody poking at it and begging to be the one to catch bugs for it and give it water and all that. Then three of the little kids started sniffling that they had broke out in warts and after that nobody would go near it. Teacher said it wasn't the toad's fault that they got the warts, 'cause toads don't give warts, although she wasn't too clear just what did.

Before we even went home for lunch, Mary Dorothy Munch found a dinky little wart on her right thumb. After lunch her hefty mother came tramping into the schoolroom, flexing her muscles and wanting to tear holes in the roof. That's when the teacher decided the toad had to go.

While the teacher was puzzling on how to get rid of the toad, Mr. John Barrow happened to walk by the schoolhouse. So she made him a present of it. She did it so nicely, he couldn't even tell her he really didn't have any use for a three-legged toad which had been his in the first place.

"Now, you take good care of the toad, Mr. John Barrow. And maybe we will ask you to come back sometime and show it to the class."

Mr. John Barrow gave the whole class a good looking over. It wasn't likely he would be too keen on coming back.

The minute the teacher turned around to write the

homework on the blackboard, Charley started kicking at his desk. He was mad, is what he was. He had paid good money for that toad, and now Mr. John Barrow had it again. The teacher turned and gave him a hard look and he stopped the kicking, but his foot kept patting on the floor.

When the lunch bell rang, Charley was the first one outside. He stomped his foot in the dirt and spit lightning and thunder. I knew what he was thinking. The teacher should've given the toad back to him if she didn't want it anymore. He started running toward Mr. John Barrow's house, with me and Sorrow close behind. He was so stirred up, I thought he might take a poke at Mr. John Barrow, but when he found him, all he did was shout.

"Mr. John Barrow, I'll give you a quarter for that toad!"

There was never a day when a toad was worth a quarter and there never would be. But it turned out Charley didn't care one bit about the money, and for all his shouting and spitting, he didn't seem too mad at Mr. John Barrow. It was the teacher he was mad at. He was going to put the toad in her desk drawer and see how *she* liked getting full of warts.

Charley took the quarter out of his pocket and held it out to Mr. John Barrow, and that was when I got the biggest shock of my whole life.

"I'm sorry, Charley," Mr. John Barrow said, "but I'm not going to sell this cute little toad. Not for any kind of money at all."

"You saving him for the Zoo Man?"

"I am not!"

"Well, what are you planning to do with the toad?" I asked him.

"I'm going to keep him. What else can I possibly do? She gave him to me, didn't she?" He was standing up taller than usual and his hand was stuck out in front of him, ready to tick off his arguments on his fingers. "Now, you jist figure it out for yourself. Why did Charley give the toad to the teacher?"

" 'Cause he was sweet on her," I told him.

"I was not!" Charley shouted at me.

"You were too!" I shouted back at him.

"Well, you see what I'm saying, don't you?" asked Mr. John Barrow. He had the look of a long, hungry cat.

"Mr. John Barrow, what do you mean?"

"The teacher's got her eye out for me, that's what. I never paid much attention to her before, but it's pretty plain she's been keeping her eye on me. She's kind of good-looking, too. Little skinny, but that don't matter too much."

At first I thought he was fooling us. Sorrow and I stood there smiling. But Charley knew he wasn't fooling right from the start and he began kicking up dirt with his hind legs, dog-fashion.

"Mr. John Barrow," he yelled, "just look at you and look at her, and I don't have to say any more!" But he kept right on going. "How could anybody in their right mind get sweet on you? Why, she had her choice of *me* and she turned it down! So, for sure you don't stand even a dead dog's chance."

Mr. John Barrow looked down at Charley and he folded his hands together like he was the preacher.

"Charley," he said, "I wish I knew you was feeling so strong about this. I'd of kept away from the teacher and saved her from herself." His voice was soft and pleasant like he was talking to a three-year-old. "But what's did is did. She showed she didn't have no use for a boy. It's more fitting she be courted by a full-growed man anyway. But I hope we can stay friends, Charley, no matter what."

He was being mighty generous about it, seeing all the encouragement he had got from the teacher so far was a three-legged toad.

"Now, you got to excuse me, 'cause I got to haul some oyster shells from Blind River over to Judge Boudreaux's. He uses them to fill up holes in his land, and he pays me pretty good for it. Then I got to go home and do some careful planning about the teacher. I got to dust off my courting clothes. I don't know that you boys ever seen me in that fine black suit my paw left me when he died. I don't wear it except at picnics and things like that."

Well, Sorrow and I have seen him in that suit. He wore it to the funeral when we buried her father. It won't help his chances much. Mr. John Barrow wears his suit like a black bedsheet on Halloween. Besides, it's got moth holes scattered all around, and the one time

I saw him in it you could see clear through to his hide, 'cause he never wears any underwear. The teacher was due for a big surprise.

But he didn't get to do his courting right away, 'cause the Zoo Man came back to town.

4

Mrs. Pauline Nix

WE WERE ABOUT ready to head back to school after lunch break when the Zoo Man walked right up on Sorrow Nix's porch and started knocking on the doorframe and yelling the door down.

"Somebody better come out here this minute! I never heard anything so stupid in my whole life. I been thinking about it practically a month. Why can't this little girl talk? She's as bright as a morning glory and prettier too!" He banged so hard on the door, the hinges rattled.

"Somebody better come out here!" he yelled.

All of a sudden he stopped his knocking and he stopped his yelling. His hand dropped to his side and he moved back a pace, ever so slowly. I could see Sorrow's mother standing behind the screen.

"Yes?" she said in a firm voice. She opened the screen door and walked out on the porch. The Zoo Man backed off even further. For the longest time he looked like he had forgotten what he came for. Then he pulled his shoulders back and started yelling again, but not so loud this time.

"Who are you?"

"My name is Mrs. Pauline Nix."

"Oh," he said. "You related to that little tyke over there?" He partly turned and pointed at Sorrow standing out in the yard.

"I'm her mother."

"Oh," he said. Something was causing him problems. "My name is Alphonse Adam Autin. They call me the Zoo Man. Maybe I better talk to your husband."

"I lost my husband," she told him. Mr. Jeremy Nix had been in the ground a whole year. Everybody in Four Corners remembers him passing.

The Zoo Man just stood there.

"You are the prettiest woman I ever seen," he said. He said it so pleasant, it didn't sound like him at all.

Mrs. Nix's hand moved up to touch her temple lightly. Then she pulled her hand back down and stuck it in her apron pocket. The Zoo Man looked at her. Then he nodded his head up and down.

"No," he said. "I didn't come here to make a fool out of myself or to pay court to a woman I only seen about thirty seconds ago." He pulled himself up tall, and his voice got loud again.

"Why did you name that beautiful child Sorrow?"

Mrs. Nix stared him down.

"If you had a daughter who couldn't talk one single word, would you name her Joy?"

His mouth opened wide. He closed it tight and didn't say a word for a whole minute. Then he started talking again.

"Mrs. Nix, it's a sinful thing that child can't talk.

Now, either you do something about it or I will.
Which is it going to be?"

Mrs. Nix stared at him. Then she smiled politely,
nodded her head slightly like she was saying "Excuse
me, please?" She walked around him, down the porch
steps and out into the yard where Sorrow stood. She
took Sorrow by the hand, nodded to me, and the two
of them walked into the side yard toward the back of
the house. The Zoo Man stood on the front porch, not
too sure what would be the right thing to do. Then he
decided and came running down the steps and into the
yard.

"Where you going?"

Mrs. Nix didn't say a word.

"Woman, you better answer me!" He walked alongside the two of them, but Mrs. Nix didn't pay him one
bit of mind.

"A doctor could fix up this little girl. You ever think
of that? She ought not to grow into a woman without being able to talk. Women were born to talk."

Mrs. Nix walked around to the back of the house,
up the steps, and in the door. She turned to lock the
door and didn't look up once. The Zoo Man ran around
front and I did too, only in time to see her lock the
front door. From that time on there wasn't a sound
coming from inside the house.

The Zoo Man stood in the front yard and yelled at
the silent house for a good long time.

"You don't have the money, I'll pay the hospital
bills," he yelled. But nobody answered.

"You scared of doctors, I'll tell you stories about doctors curing people that'll make you want to fry them a ten-course meal," he yelled.

For the longest time he just stood there.

"You have to at least try, woman. That child's got a right to a chance at talking."

But the house stayed silent.

Finally, he glanced at me, looked at the ground, turned around and walked to the road. He kicked up the dirt as he walked. When he got to the road he reached down quick, picked up a rock, turned around and hurled it at the house. It thumped on top of the roof.

"I'm coming back, and I'm going to yell some more," he yelled.

5

Singing

I HAD NEVER thought much about why Sorrow couldn't talk. After school I asked my dad about it and he said he didn't know either.

"But I tell you one thing," he said. "When that child was just a tot, her maw and paw spent more time hauling her to city hospitals than the law allows. If there was something that could've been done, it would've been done. I don't think it's a good idea for that stranger to start sticking his nose into things that ain't none of his business. All that'll happen is he's going to stir up Sorrow. She's a happy little girl. She don't need stirring up."

But the Zoo Man got Sorrow to thinking. I didn't bring the subject up. She did. She came over after supper and made me sit on the porch steps and listen.

"I *can* talk," she wrote. "Better than some. Making sounds is only part of talking."

I was so used to her not talking that I didn't know what to say. But it was true. Mr. John Barrow does more sound-making than talking.

Sorrow and I talked about it for a long time. She was writing furiously, and I leaned over to read the words as soon as she had finished them.

"Most of the time I don't mind," she wrote. "I like writing about what I think and what I feel. And Momma has taught me to dance pretty good." She stopped writing for a minute and stared out into space. Then the words started tumbling out again. "If I really get mad, I can make a fist and pound on something. Most times I pound on my mattress or I find a soft piece of dirt." She looked at me with a tiny smile and I smiled back.

"But sometimes I get so furious!" She told me about the time she smacked an iron pot and her knuckles got skinned. "They turned black and blue and I had shooting pains in them for a week." She rubbed her knuckles like they were still sore.

"When my paw died, I could barely hold the feeling inside me. You helped me, Pinch. Just being there. Just knowing you didn't expect me to say a single word. Telling me stories and giving me presents. You were a good friend. You still are." She stared at me.

Sorrow is a pretty thing. Her eyes are brown and big. Her nose is thin and straight. She started to sniffle. There was a little smile on her lips, but the smile was twitching and wouldn't be there too much longer.

She picked up a twig off the ground and twiddled with it. She looked at me. There was something more she wanted to tell me. She looked up at the winter sky. A bird circled way up high.

Wanting to help and not being able to help is the worst feeling in the whole wide world.

Then she started to write again.

"It's when I'm happy that it hurts. It's when I just *have* to yell for joy. It's more than smiling or dancing or jumping up and down. It's more important than that.

Things inside me want to spill out and I don't know how to get them out." She was quiet again. She bent back to the paper and spelled the letters out ever so slowly.

"Pinch, what's it feel like to sing?"

6

The Willow Whistle

I GOT UP EARLY the next morning and ate a fast breakfast. I wanted to talk to Sorrow. I hadn't slept too well. I wanted to tell her that talking's not everything. There are plenty of things more important than talking. I hoped I could think of one before I got to her house.

Dad was sitting on the front steps.

"Pinch, look here what I'm doing."

It was the willow whistle. Last spring he had promised me one. He had even started on it. He had cut off a piece of willow about as long as his hand and soaked it in water. He had rolled it around on the ground and pounded on it to loosen the bark from the wood.

"You see what I'm doing?" he asked then. He had cut off enough bark on one end so he could grab hold of the wood. He held the piece of willow in both hands, one twisting the bark, one holding firm on the wood.

Pop! Out came the wood. He was holding onto a hollow piece of willow bark.

Right then Mom had yelled for us to come and eat and that was the end of him making my willow whistle. But now he was at it again.

"You watch what I do, Pinch, and next time you can do it yourself."

He cut a perfectly round piece of wood from a dry willow branch and plugged it into one end of the hollow willow bark.

"Pinch, something very interesting happened this morning when I was walking my trapping line. I saw a big white crane on the river. First time I ever saw one so big." He was looking at the whistle, but he had stopped working on it. "Son, when my paw was just a boy, there were dozens of big white cranes around here every winter. My paw saw them, Pinch. Some of those birds were here all year long." He had forgotten all about the whistle. "Some went off someplace in the summer. My paw said the little ones were brown and the big ones were white. How you like that, Pinch? Maybe the little ones can hide better, being brown. But it's a kind of miracle, son."

He stared out into the yard where the big oak grew. It was my favorite tree. I swing from its rope swing and I climb from its twisted branches. Then he looked down at his hands. He cut another round plug out of the willow. This time he flattened out the top of it so that air could flow through.

"Dozens of them, Pinch. But all of them are gone now. Hasn't been a big crane around Four Corners since my paw was a boy. They are a very special bird. Not too many left any place at all."

He looked down at his hands, and it was like he had forgotten the willow whistle again. He put the knife down on the porch and rubbed his fingers over the bark. He put the whistle to his mouth and blew. The air filled the whistle but there was no sound.

"It's airtight. So far, so good." He cut a notch into the barrel of the whistle and shaved at it until he had it just the way he wanted it. Then he put it to his lips one more time.

"Whhhhhooooo!"

It was a sharp sound and it was a soft sound at the same time.

"There," he said, and handed it to me. "Keep an eye out for the big white crane, Pinch. It's something special to see."

I took a happy walk to Sorrow's house.

"You ever see a willow whistle?" I handed it to her.

"Whhhhhooooo! Whhhhhooooo! Whhhhhooooo!" she tooted. She liked the sweet sound and she liked being able to make the noise.

"My dad made it for us," I told her. "You keep it for now."

7

The Armadillo

WHEN I GOT HOME that afternoon Dad and Mr. Tony Carmouche were crowded around a wire cage in our back yard. Mr. Tony is the only storekeeper in Four Corners and sometimes I do deliveries for him. His store is right across the road from our house. He is a small, wiry man and smarter than most folks in town. You want to know anything that you can find in books, you ask him. He'll know it. He is also the deputy sheriff, but Four Corners doesn't give him too much sheriffing business.

The cage was for rabbits. My dad traps rabbits whenever he can get them. They are good eating. Sometimes he catches a skunk or a possum and cages them for a few days so we can look at them. He gives them a cleaning or patches up their scratches. They generally won't eat. They just walk around, testing the wire, and maybe hissing or moaning. When he has studied them a while, he turns them loose.

"Pinch, come take a look at this rascal. Don't get to see too many of them around here."

It was an armadillo. They are funny-looking animals and plenty of them are running loose, but I never saw one up close before. They run and dig so fast, they don't let you get close to them.

Right then the Zoo Man came walking across the yard and joined them at the cage.

"Funniest thing you ever saw," Dad said. "He was sunning himself, belly up. I just snuck up and put a sack over him and that's all there was to it."

The Zoo Man had his head up close to the cage.

"Mr. Grimball, you want to sell this animal, I'd probably buy it if the price was fair."

"Well, I don't know. I ain't much on animals in cages."

"I tell you what I would do, Will Grimball," said Mr. Tony Carmouche. "I'd fry it. I never ate one myself, but I been told they are tastier than rabbit. I can't offer you any advice on how to get it out of the shell, but there's got to be a way."

I was listening, but I didn't like what I was hearing. We had been trapping and eating rabbits all my life, and I was used to it. Rabbits are good tasting. But I wasn't too keen on keeping them for pets. I tried it once. Me and Dad built a great big chicken-wire pen. We even sunk the wire down into the ground about a foot so they couldn't dig their way out. Then the next time he caught a rabbit we dumped it into the pen. There was plenty of grass, and we threw in a pile of table scraps. First it ate up all the live grass. Then it would sit and wait until we came by with the table scraps. Mostly it sat and looked outside. Then one day it died. Dad said it probably got the worms. But I think maybe it was from spending all of its time looking at the live grass outside of the cage and not being able to reach it.

I never tried to do it again. We stuck a pile of chickens in the pen. They were happy there. They laid their eggs and clucked and crowed. They weren't interested in roaming in the fields where a dog could get at them. Chickens can't hardly make it on their own. Maybe one time they could, but they don't want to anymore. Rabbits are different. They can hear good and they can run good, and they are ready to take their chances.

The armadillo stared out at me, sending me a message. This ain't where I want to be, it was saying.

"Well, I could use this animal," the Zoo Man said. "Had one once. Those critters are easy to keep. You got to give them some mud to dig into, but that's about all. They don't eat nothing but insects, so they're cheap. You decide to sell, you let me know."

"Don't think I will," Dad said.

"You decide to cook it, I'd like a taste," said Mr. Tony Carmouche.

"Don't think I'll do that either," Dad said. "Now, you excuse me for a minute," he said. He walked over to the house and called for Mom to come out and take a look at the armadillo.

I took the chance to ask the Zoo Man a question.

"You interested in buying a three-legged toad frog?" Mr. John Barrow might still sell it if the profit was high enough.

"Scat!" he yelled. "Toads ain't animals. Toads is toads!"

When Mom came out Sorrow was with her. Mom brought an overripe banana and when she poked it in the cage the little animal showed its first sign of being happy. He nipped away at the banana until he had finished off about half of it. Didn't seem to mind all of us watching.

"Tony," Dad said, "the weather is nice. I been doing pretty good on my trapping lines. Why don't you and the missus come over after supper. We'll have a party. I'll even throw in some cider I got hid away, if it ain't turned sour." The Zoo Man had stopped looking at the armadillo and was staring at Dad. "You come too, Mr. Autin. I don't know a thing about zoo keeping. Probably don't need to know much. But we can chat."

"I'll be there." He nodded a thank-you. "But I can't stay late. I saw a big white crane flying down near the river. I got to go crane hunting first thing in the morning."

Dad stared hard at him. "I saw that crane too, and it don't belong in a cage!" They were angry words.

The Zoo Man stared back. "I got to make a living, same as you."

Dad simmered down. "You going near Blind River?"

"Thought I would."

"Well, I don't want to sound unhospitable, but don't go near the boats at the dock. They've been out of the water for months and are full of leaks. Some even got rot in them."

"Thank you for the warning," the Zoo Man said. Then he nodded his good-byes all around and walked toward the gate.

I had no idea then all the trouble the big white crane would bring.

8

Time for a Party

EVERYBODY CAME to the party. There was plenty of pound cake and cider. And singing. Whenever there's a party, my mom likes to sing.

"Who knows 'You Are My Sunshine'? "

Everybody did.

"Be quiet, everybody," Mr. John Barrow raised his skinny hands over his head. "You want to hear a real good song, jist listen to this." He has a high, squeaky voice that nobody likes to hear, but that doesn't seem to bother him any. "This was my paw's favorite song."

> *It's not that I don't love you,*
> *It's not that I don't care,*
> *It's just I can't go courting*
> *With holes in my underwear.*

Mom stood up and started clapping her hands.

"Very good, very good!"

"But I ain't finished singing."

"Yes you have, John. I would've thought a grown

man would've known better than to sing a song like that with these children sitting here."

The Zoo Man had been taking it all in without saying a word. It didn't look like he was having too much fun, but maybe he was. This time it was him that stood up.

"I don't understand you people. You don't know how to have a good time. Now, you listen to this. I'm going to sing you a song that'll get things going like they ought to. It's a long one, but I'll only sing a little bit." He cleared his throat and started singing. He had a deep, clear voice, but I didn't find anything to laugh at in his song.

Cows gone dry and hens won't lay
Fish quit bitin' last Saturday
Troubles pile up day by day
And now I'm gittin dandruff.

"Now that's what I call singing," said Mr. John Barrow, clapping his hands, but the Zoo Man gave him such a hard stare, he shut up quick.

Grief and misery, pain and woes
Debts and taxes and so it goes
And I think I'm gittin' a cold in the nose
Life gits tasteless, don't it?

"We got enough of that," Mom said before he had a chance to sing any more. "What we need is a little sweetness and light if this is going to keep being a party. Now, we are going to stop singing foolish songs and sing 'Sunshine.' " She looked at Mr. John Barrow and at the Zoo Man. "You two hear me?" They nodded they did.

"All right, everybody," Mr. John Barrow said, getting on his feet again, "when I count three, we will start."

"Sit down, John, we don't need a leader," Mom told him. But Mr. John Barrow looked so sad at not being able to be the leader that she changed her mind.

"I tell you what, John. You just stomp your foot three times, and then we will start."

You are my sunshine, my only sunshine
You make me happy when skies are gray
You'll never know, dear, how much I love you
Please don't take my sunshine away.

You couldn't call it singing, but it was fun. Mom was standing, her head tilted to the ceiling, screeching away. She just loved to sing.

You told me once, dear, you really loved me . . .

My dad was sitting over in the corner, mumbling. He is never happy when he is singing. Mr. Tony Carmouche has a kind of thin, pretty voice. I got to say I like to hear him sing.

And no one else could come between . . .

Mr. John Barrow was doing more arm waving than singing, but his rickety voice made more noise than anybody else in the room. He was having the time of his life.

But now you've left me and love another . . .

I looked over at Sorrow to see if she was having as good a time as I was. Her eyes were sparkling in the firelight. Her head was high. She mouthed the words, even though no sound came.

You have shattered all my dreams.

I was having so much fun, the song ended too soon.

"Now, that's what I call singing," Mr. John Barrow said. He looked all around the room to see if everybody agreed with him.

"Will Grimball, you could do better if you tried," he said, looking over at my dad. "And Mr. Autin, you ain't singing at all." He pointed a finger at the Zoo Man, but when the Zoo Man turned his head and stared at him, Mr. John Barrow shifted his eyes to another part of the room and landed on Sorrow.

"Hello, Sorrow," he waved. "Sorry you can't sing the words with us."

Sometimes Mr. John Barrow doesn't think too good. Sorrow had been having as good a time as anybody until that very moment. She looked at him. She looked down at the floor. Her mouth closed.

"All right, now, let's sing it again," Mom said.

The other night, dear, as I lay sleeping . . .

But I didn't join in. I watched Sorrow. She stared at the floor. I looked around the room to see if anybody else saw what Mr. John Barrow had done. When I looked back for Sorrow, she wasn't there anymore.

Mr. John Barrow hadn't noticed. Nobody else had, either. Only me.

The singing got sweeter, it got louder. Everybody was yelling away and having the best time of their lives. Except us.

Sorrow was off somewhere by herself. There was no way I could be happy knowing that. I even quit mumbling the words.

Please don't take my sunshine away.

The song ended. There was clapping and foot stomping. Then there was a moment of silence and another sound came.

"Whhhhhooooo!"

It was the willow whistle. The front door burst open and Sorrow came marching into the room.

"Whhhhhooooo!"

We watched her. Nobody but me knew that she hadn't been with us right along. Even Mr. John Barrow didn't know the harm he had done.

She marched around the room. She tooted on her willow whistle all the while. Knees up high! Slam down foot! She was marching!

She stopped. She smiled. It was a smile that made everybody in the room wish they could smile so good. She started marching again, straight over to Mr. John

Barrow and tucked her arm in his. He had hurt her but he hadn't meant to. She knew that. She handed him the willow whistle. He gave her a big grin and started tooting on the whistle like he was the best whistle tooter in the whole wide world. Mr. John Barrow was as happy as a puppy dog.

The two of them marched around the room, arm in arm, then out the front door. We heard them tooting. It was sharp at first. Then it got dimmer. Then we couldn't hear it anymore.

9

Sorrow's Crane

WHEN I STOPPED for Sorrow on the way to school the next morning, she wasn't sitting on the porch waiting like she usually is.

I yelled for her to come out but her mom stuck her head out the door and said I should go ahead. Sorrow had gone over to Blind River and would be a little late.

I went looking, and when I found her she was sitting on the river bank, colored pencil in hand, drawing on a piece of white cardboard. That's when I remembered why she was here. Today was her turn to talk to the class. She always did it the same way. She showed us her drawings and she told us things about them by writing on the blackboard. I couldn't see what she was drawing. I stepped closer, a twig snapped, and her head turned quick. She put a finger to her lips.

There were two cranes in the shallow water down the bank a ways. They were feeding. One was the largest, most beautiful crane I had ever seen. It was taller than I was and pure white. There was a red crown on its head. The other wasn't near so big, and there was creamy brown mixed in with the white. They looked alike, and yet they didn't.

Sorrow smiled up at me. The bird on her drawing board was even more beautiful than the bird in the water. She had drawn the biggest of the two cranes, with its long yellow-gray bill dipped down in the water. I heard a sound. I looked up. The big crane snapped at a small fish, crushed it, swallowed, then lifted its long black legs and moved a step away. It walked like a queen in court. Its head moved side to side in stiff, jerky movements, looking for another tasty fish.

We hadn't made a single sound. Suddenly the crane sensed something. Its head turned in our direction. Yellow eyes stared at the tiny bit of me and Sorrow that showed. The stare sent shivers through me. That big crane didn't know me. It didn't want to know me. Its eyes were telling me this.

It turned and walked toward the smaller crane, nudging it with its head, telling it to move away from danger. The little brown and white crane was skinny-legged and sad-eyed. It was helpless-looking. The two birds stood close together, not making a sound. They were telling each other things by touching. Then the big crane straightened. It turned and stared at us.

"Stay away!" it was saying.

Then it turned its back on us and started a slow walk down the shoreline. The walk got faster. Huge, black-tipped wings lifted into the air.

"Ker-loo!" it called. It was like the sound of a bugle, only sweeter and softer. It flew out over the river and then circled back again.

The small crane's head popped up and it moved quickly through the shallow water. Its brown wings lifted out, but suddenly one wing dropped, the tip trailing in the water as it ran. The wing of the little crane was tipped in satiny black, just like the big crane. It was as though it was wearing winter mittens. But one of its mittens hung limp.

The little crane wanted desperately to fly. It wanted to follow the big crane. It tried again and again, but one-winged birds don't fly.

Sorrow's thin face was paper white. She wanted to go to the crane and touch its wing and heal it that very moment.

The shore of Blind River was a good hiding place for a crane with a hurt wing. Not too many people went there, especially not when the weather was cold. But there was danger, too. The crane was hemmed in by deep water on one side and swamp on the other. It was a cage for a bird who couldn't fly. Now there was plenty of food available. But the weather was going to get colder and I didn't know if the fish and whatever else that bird ate would stay around until the wing healed.

Sorrow stood there, watching the crane. There was pain on her face.

"Maybe you could fix the wing if we caught it," I

told her. She looked quickly at me and smiled. It was a good idea.

I had never caught a crane before. And running after one in freezing cold winter water wasn't my idea of the best way to do it.

"Let's come back after school. We can bring some corn and tempt it out of the water. Then we can grab it."

We moved away from the bank as quietly as we could. The real crane stayed in the water. The picture crane was tucked under Sorrow's arm. I hoped some bird hunter didn't creep up on the little crane while we were gone.

And then I remembered.

This was the morning the Zoo Man said he would start looking for the big white crane.

10

Return of the Toad

THE SCHOOLTEACHER didn't hardly let us sit down before she started collecting homework. There are two times in school I really hate. One is when the teacher collects homework you didn't get a chance to do. The other is getting called on when you don't know the answer.

"Where's your drawing, Pinch?" the teacher asked.

"I accidentally forgot," I told her. "It was chores is what it was."

"Class, I want you to see Sorrow's drawing. I'll put it here on the board." She held it up for all the kids to see. They started making bird sounds and poking fun, but nobody was being really mean about it, 'cause they all liked Sorrow and every one of them wished they could draw half as well.

"You know the name of this bird?" the teacher asked.

Sorrow went to the blackboard. "It's a crane," she wrote.

"You know what kind of crane it is?"

Sorrow shook her head. Her mind wasn't really on

the big white crane. It was on the little brown one with the broken wing that was out there all alone.

"Sorrow, when you go home, you take a closer look at the picture you were copying. There ought to be a name written under the picture. Tomorrow you can tell us the name of the bird."

But there wasn't any picture to get the name from. And for sure Sorrow didn't want the kids to learn there were two live cranes over by Blind River and only one of them could fly. All the kids would be throwing rocks ten minutes after school was out.

The schoolteacher took the drawing and thumb-tacked it on the wall with the others the class had drawn. It stuck out. Sorrow's drawings always stick out. The yellow-eyed crane stared at us, daring us to stare it back.

I looked at Sorrow. I hadn't told her that the Zoo Man was out there hunting, and I wasn't planning to tell her. We would try to catch the little crane after school. Tomorrow Sorrow would have to tell the teacher she didn't know what kind of crane it was. If the teacher *really* wanted to know more, Sorrow could show her the baby crane. She trusted the teacher. But this wasn't the time for telling.

We were about to settle into arithmetic when Mr. John Barrow poked his head in the front door.

"Teacher? Could I talk with you for jist a minute?"

"Mr. John Barrow, we are trying to learn our arith-metic."

He came into the classroom. He had the toad box in his hand.

"Won't take a minute, I promise. I jist wondered if the children would like to have the toad back for a day or so?"

The little kids with warts started sniffling and the teacher stood up and walked over to their side of the room.

"Thank you, but I think not. He's yours to keep and care for."

"All right, then," he said, "but my sleep ain't been the same since that toad's been around." He started to leave. Then his eyes moved to the wall where all the drawings were. Something caught his eye and he squinted and moved closer.

"What kind of bird is that?" he asked the teacher. He was looking at Sorrow's drawing of the crane.

"We don't know, Mr. John Barrow. Maybe you can help us find out."

"It's a crane," he said.

"We figured it, Mr. John Barrow. But what kind of crane do you suppose it is?"

He puzzled on it. "I seen cranes like that when I was a boy. Don't have them around here no more. Who drew the pretty picture?"

"Sorrow."

He turned and looked at Sorrow. Mr. John Barrow and Sorrow are special friends. He never once tried pulling any of his bargaining tricks on her.

"Hello, Sorrow," he smiled at her. "You seen this bird or you git it out of a picture book?"

He stared at Sorrow and she stared back, but not a sound passed between them.

"Sorrow's going to look up the name of the bird in the book and tell us," the teacher said.

"Oh." Mr. John Barrow was still waiting for Sorrow to answer his question, but she never did. When he got tired waiting, he turned back to the teacher and nodded.

"The Zoo Man is out near Blind River looking for animals this very minute. Maybe he'll find himself a big yellow-eyed crane after all." He gave a kind of sideways look at Sorrow. Then he shifted his eyes back to the teacher.

"I thank you for the nice present you gave me," he said, jiggling the toad. Then he left.

I turned quickly to Sorrow. She was staring straight at me. There was more than half a day of school before we could start trying to catch the little crane.

11

Arithmetic

MR. JOHN BARROW wasn't gone five minutes when Henry and Billy Sweet poked their heads in the door.

"Can we come in?"

"We are trying to learn our arithmetic," she told them. But they just came on in anyway.

Billy and Henry are both grown men, but most of the time they don't act like it. Billy is the skinny one. He doesn't even have a wife like Henry does. I don't exactly know what Billy does for a living. I never see him work much. He does a little whiskey drinking. Sometimes he chops wood. And he's kind of mean. All those things. You can double most of that for his brother Henry. Henry is kind of fat. His wife is medium. The one thing different is Henry's got a piece of a job care-taking on Judge Boudreaux's farm. Doesn't work too hard at it though.

It looked like Billy Sweet heard about all the atten-tion Mr. John Barrow was talking about giving the schoolteacher and decided to give her a looking over himself. Billy didn't really have a chance, 'cause he doesn't have one brain in his head. I guess he figured any man that was smart enough to get along without doing a stick of work who could still eat three full meals a day just had to be a pretty smart fellow.

So he came to call on her, and to show you just how smart he was, he did it in the middle of the school day when all of us kids could watch, and he brought his brother Henry along with him.

The teacher came from behind her desk to see what they wanted. She was too nice to yell at them to go away.

"What can I do for you two boys?"

Billy looked at Henry and Henry looked at Billy, and both of them sort of chuckled but didn't say anything.

"We have an arithmetic class about to start. Not much time to talk."

"Har, har, har," said Billy, kicking at the floor. He's not exactly a shy one most of the time, but this time he was. Henry was doing his own giggling, but he stopped and looked at the teacher.

"Billy was wondering if you would have some time this evening to . . . ahh . . . to teach him some arithmetic." He gave a quick look over at Billy and both of them started giggling real loud and stomping their feet.

"I see," said the teacher. "What kind of arithmetic are we talking about?"

"Twelve times twelve!" Charley Riedlinger shouted.

The teacher looked over at him and kind of shushed him quiet with her hand.

"That's not it," Henry said, and Billy grinned and shook his head side to side like he knew what the answer was too. "Everybody knows what twelve times twelve is, 'cept maybe dumb little crooked-nosed kids." He looked square at Charley.

"Well, what is it then?" Charley yelled at him.

Billy and Henry hadn't come here for a quizzing. Henry turned back to the teacher, figuring he would act like he never heard Charley. But the teacher is always one who is looking to teach.

"Charley Riedlinger," she said, "let's hear what twelve times twelve is for the two Mr. Sweets."

I'm pretty sure Charley knew the answer, but it was easy to see Charley was pretty sure the Sweet boys didn't know it, and he was going to find out.

"Him first," Charley said.

Billy still wasn't doing anything but grinning, although it wasn't as big a grin as when all this started. Henry looked mean. He kind of hunched his body forward and made fists with each hand.

"Twelve times twelve is a hundred and something," he said, sticking his chin out front. "Now, I don't want to hear no more about twelve times twelve."

The teacher smiled just a little bit. She looked from Henry to Billy.

"Billy Sweet, how much is twelve times twelve?"

"Har, har, har," said Billy. It was the best joke he had

ever heard. He slid his feet around in the dirt and looked over at Henry and looked back at the teacher. He kept up his har-har-har all the while. It was like he was trying to fill up the whole world with laughing sounds.

The schoolteacher finally agreed to teach some arithmetic to Billy after school. She said she would do it if Henry came too. And she said they would start with one plus one instead of twelve times twelve.

"Har, har, har," said Billy. "That's a pretty good place to start."

"You boys come to my desk for a minute and I'll give you some lesson books."

They weren't up in front of the classroom two seconds when Billy's eye lit on Sorrow's drawing of the big crane.

"What kind of bird is that?" he asked.

"Got no idea," the teacher said. She handed each of them a book. "Now, you look over lesson one, and you come back after school lets out and we will start."

"It looks like a big crane," Billy said. "My paw used to call them hoopers. Tasty as a Christmas turkey. Who did the pretty drawing?"

"It was Sorrow. Now I got to start class, so you boys got to leave."

"Wouldn't mind finding a bird like that," Billy said as they started out the door. "Fact is, I'm getting hungry just thinking about it." He turned back and looked Sorrow square in the eye.

"Where should I start looking, Sorrow?"

The two of them giggled again, then turned around and left. But Sorrow wasn't giggling. The little crane's chances were getting smaller by the minute.

When the bell rang I bolted for the door, but the teacher stopped me.

"Your turn with the erasers, young man."

I looked toward Sorrow. Her shoulders dropped. It was as though everything was happening to make certain the little crane ended up in a zoo.

"Teacher, could I clean the erasers in the morning?"

"No."

"Could I skip today and do them for a week?"

"No."

I looked at Sorrow with a question on my face and when she nodded I started talking to the teacher about how important it was that Sorrow and I get to Blind River. But right then Henry and Billy Sweet walked up the front steps, grinning like old pokey hounds. I stopped talking.

"Wait for me at your house, Sorrow."

12

The Crane Drawing

THE ONE THING the Sweets didn't like when they were learning numbers was any little kids around. But the teacher told them not to pay me any mind. While I erased the board, I had part of my mind on Sorrow and the crane. I had to hurry. Maybe no one had found it yet. We were the only ones who knew where to look. But where would we put it if we caught it? It had to be a place where no one could find it. I tried to think, but there was too much foolishness going on in the rear of the room.

"Henry, suppose you had six apples and Billy had six apples and I had six apples. How many apples would we have?"

"That's a lot of apples," Henry said.

Billy hadn't done much talking to the teacher at first. But once the arithmetic lessons started, he spilled words out all over the place. The trouble was Billy was more interested in the teacher than he was in learning arithmetic.

"What would we do with the apples?" Billy asked.

"Hello!" somebody yelled from outside the front door.

It was the Zoo Man! I knew it! He was coming to tell us he had caught the crane!

He pulled the door open and stuck his head inside.

"What's going on in here?" he asked.

"Come in," said the teacher.

He did. He looked all around, giving the Sweets a hard look. Then he saw me washing down the blackboard with a damp rag.

"Hi, boy," he said. I nodded to him. He turned and looked at the schoolteacher.

"You the schoolteacher?" he asked, kind of like he dared her to deny it.

"What can I do for you?" she asked him pleasantly.

"Well, I'll tell you." He looked first at me, then back at her. "I'm trying to find out why that little girl can't talk. What can you tell me about that?"

"Thought you were crane hunting," Billy Sweet said.

"Can't hunt cranes all day long," the Zoo Man told him.

By that time he had walked straight up to the teacher and was standing next to her. He was a pushy man, that was for sure, always ready to stick his nose into something else that didn't concern him. He didn't pay another particle of attention to the Sweet boys. Looked right over their heads like they weren't there.

The schoolteacher stared like she wasn't sure what to do at first. Then she stood up. She only came up to his shoulders, but she has a way of staring at you that keeps you to her size.

"I don't know your name," she told him.

"I'm the Zoo Man," he told her.

"That ain't much of a name," Henry Sweet said.

"I ain't asking you nothing," the Zoo Man turned and yelled at him. He switched to standing over Henry, teeth clenched, like he was waiting for Henry to say one more word. When Henry didn't, he turned to the teacher again.

"I was baptized Alphonse Adam Autin, but that don't make no difference. Nobody calls me that. They call me the Zoo Man."

"Well, Mr. Autin, you sit down." She poked a finger at his chest. "Right there." She pointed at a school desk that was about half his size. I didn't expect him to do what he was told, but the Zoo Man sat down in the desk like the teacher told him to. It was like trying to stuff a pan-sized perch into a sardine can.

"Now, let's talk," she said, "but for a little while you listen and I'll do the talking." She stared at him and kept staring until he nodded he understood.

"I know a few things you ought to know," the school-teacher said to him. "I know Sorrow's mother and father tried everything in their power to make her talk. They went to the best doctors they could find. Nothing worked. Finally they taught Sorrow to make the best use of what she had. That's all any of us should be asked to do." She looked at him. But she wasn't finished.

"Mr. Zoo Man, or whatever your name is, Sorrow Nix is more normal than the two of us. Don't you do anything that will make her feel otherwise." The teacher stood beside her desk. It was a step higher than the regular classroom. But she looked higher still and the Zoo Man could see it. At first he didn't have another word to say. Then he looked straight at her.

"Lady, I'm going to tell you one thing and then I'm going to walk right out of here." He took a breath and mumbled something we couldn't hear.

"Mmmmmmaaaaa."

"What's that, Mr. Autin?" the teacher asked.

He was having a hard time telling it.

"My maw," he said, kind of low. "My maw couldn't walk one single step her last twenty years. It was me who took care of her, day to day." He looked away from her, then back again. He rubbed his shirt-sleeve back and forth against his nose. "A bubbly woman," he said softly. He looked over at the Sweets. He wasn't happy that they were listening, but they were quiet and hanging on every word. He looked back at the teacher and his voice got loud again.

"I take good care of my animals," he said. "You know how long I been putting up with that durned fool one-eyed turkey?" His eyes roamed around the room again. He looked at the windows and the walls. He looked at the drawings the kids had made. Then his eyes stopped roaming. He stared at something. I followed his eyes. It was Sorrow's picture of the crane.

"What's that?" he asked.

"It's a drawing," the teacher said.

"I can see that. What's it supposed to be a drawing of?"

"It's a crane. Don't know what kind. We don't have cranes like that around here."

"Well, I think I seen one on Blind River just this afternoon," Henry said. "It was kind of like that big bird, for sure. We took a shot at it but we missed."

The Zoo Man glared at Henry, not saying a word. Then he turned suddenly and walked out of the schoolroom, feet pounding loud on the board floor. Something had grabbed tight on his mind. Something about the crane that we didn't know.

13

The Question

NO ONE FOLLOWED Sorrow and me down the road toward Blind River. When we got close, we stopped by a big oak tree and waited. I looked behind and to all sides. We seemed to be alone, but there were so many other trees and shadows, someone could be watching from anywhere.

We crossed the little levee. The big white crane was nowhere to be seen. The small brownish crane was down the shoreline a ways, feeding in some marsh grass. You had to look good to see it.

We put a trail of corn on the shore and I ducked behind some sticker bushes. Sorrow put on wading boots and moved slowly out into the water beyond the crane. It saw her coming and stopped feeding. Then Sorrow started chasing it to shore. When the crane saw the corn it slowed down and I flipped the sack. That was it! We had a squawking, unhappy bird in a burlap sack. It weighed about as much as a watermelon so it wasn't too hard to carry. At least not for the first quarter mile. Then, before my arms fell off, Sorrow stopped me and grabbed hold of one part of the sack. We made a kind

of hammock out of it, her holding up the front end and me the back.

We snuck around behind Sorrow's house and strung chicken wire around some trees in the woods. Wasn't likely anyone would be looking back there. We checked the bird's wing before turning it loose. There wasn't anything broken. One wing was bent kind of funny. I was thinking maybe this bird just wasn't meant to fly.

Sorrow thought different.

"The wing will mend," she wrote me. "I know it."

She tried being friendly with the crane. She threw it a handful of corn, but it didn't pay one bit of attention to the corn. It just stood there, watching.

It wouldn't eat. It wouldn't let us come near. That's the way it stayed for about three days. Then one morning early we came up on it scratching in the dirt for grubs. When Sorrow threw it a handful of acorns, it gobbled them so fast, you could almost count the acorns slipping down its long neck, heading toward its craw. After that we had to work hard to feed it. Most evenings Sorrow put me to work walking the shore of Blind River, catching little fish and crabs with a scoop net. She figured the crane needed a treat once in a while.

Things were nice. Nobody came by. The crane was safe. Sorrow was happy. It stayed like that for about a week. The Zoo Man and the Sweets and Mr. John Barrow and everybody's cousin kept looking for a big white crane on Blind River. Nobody looked for a little brown crane in the woods behind Sorrow's house.

We took good care of the crane. The trouble is, that's all we did. Find acorns and catch little fish! That's all Sorrow wanted to do. I had really started to like the crane, but chores is chores, even when you're doing them for Sorrow's crane.

"Sorrow, let's take a walk to Red Bluff and see if we can find some arrowheads?" I asked her. She picked up the bent bucket we kept the little fish in and put it in my hand. But I put it down on the ground.

"I'm not going to do it!" I told her. "I'm tired of messing with that crane. It was fun for a while, but it's not fun anymore."

She tilted her head kind of sideways, like the crane did when it was puzzled. I stared straight at her, but I never was too good at saying no to Sorrow. So I pretty quick stopped staring.

"I'm going to see if Charley wants to find some arrowheads," I told her. And I left.

I didn't want to find arrowheads. I mean, maybe I did, but that wasn't the main thing. It's not doing things. It's who you do things with. Charley is pretty nice. At least some of the time. But it's not the same hunting arrowheads with Charley and hunting arrowheads with Sorrow. I don't know why that is. My dad didn't either. I know he didn't, 'cause on the morning of the third day that I stayed away from Sorrow and the crane, him and me had a talk in the kitchen.

"Dad?" He was fixing the water faucet. He is always fixing something. "Are boys different from girls?"

"What's that, Pinch?" He stopped his fixing and looked at me.

"I been thinking."

"Nothing unusual about that, son."

"Sorrow's spending so much time tending to things she wants to do that she and I don't do anything together any more. Me and Charley have been spending a lot of time together. We've been looking for arrowheads and fishing, and things like that. But something's different about it."

"What's that, son?"

"I don't know. That's what I want to talk about. Is there something different about boys from girls?"

"Pinch, you and I already talked about that."

"I remember, but that's not what I'm asking about." The problem was I didn't know the right question to ask.

"Dad, why did you marry Mom?"

His head popped up from what he was fixing.

"What's that, Pinch?" But he had heard me. He looked at me straight in the eye. He was trying to find out what I really was asking him. I didn't know. All I really knew was there was something special about just being around Sorrow Nix. Me and Charley would laugh and stomp and kick around. It was fun, but it wasn't really special.

"Pinch, I wonder if you would do me a favor?"

"What's that?"

"Go talk to your mom."

You got to understand my dad. When it's outside things, he knows what he is doing. When it's inside things, he is not quite so sure. Shaking of hands is something my dad knows pretty good. He holds onto your hand like a wood vise. Kissing on cheeks is something my mom knows better. Her kisses are softer than a butterfly's nose.

14

A Kind of Glowing

MOM WAS IN THE front room sewing. She was making a patchwork quilt. I kind of like the colors in them. She uses my old britches and my old shirts and anything else around the house that has been outgrown or has too many holes to be fixed.

"Hi, Mom."

"Hello, Pinch."

"Mom, are boys different from girls?"

"You bet your boots they are." She looked up from her sewing and smiled at me. "I got two boys, Pinch. One is growed, and the other is working on it. And I'd trade you both for Sorrow Nix."

"Thanks a lot, Mom."

"Son, I'm just partial to little girls. The way I look at it is the Lord made Adam and then when he got ready to make Eve, he knew a little more about what he was doing."

"I'm serious, Mom."

"All right, Pinch, then I will try to be serious too."

"I want to talk about Sorrow."

She put down her scissors and the cloth, put her hands in her lap, and looked straight at me.

"You have my full attention."

I told her about the crane. I told her she couldn't tell anybody 'cause we surely didn't want that little brown crane to end up in a zoo or on the Sweets' dinner table. And I told her how Sorrow has been so busy with the crane that we don't get to do anything else but chores.

"Mom, me and Charley have been hunting for arrowheads and looking for crawfish. We even cut some bamboo and made popguns out of it. I'm getting tired of all that stuff. I'm not having as much fun as I used to have before Sorrow started tending to the crane."

Mom looked at me. She nodded her head to one side, telling me to sit down on the chair next to her. She held out one soft hand. It stuck out there. The hand was telling me to put my hand in hers, so I did.

"Pinch, you are asking one of the hardest questions there is. The answer is easy. Sure, there's plenty difference between boys and girls. For a fact, there is plenty difference between Sorrow and Charley. But when you get past saying that Sorrow is pretty and Charley's nose is kind of tilted sideways, the going gets hard." She thought about it some. "Son, I really don't think I know the answer. But I'm going to give you some things to think about." She picked up her scissors and a piece of cloth that used to be a blue dress for city shopping.

"I think the answer has something to do with gentleness. They call men gentlemen, but I never seen one.

They are rough. All of them. I got a notion it's country living that does it, so maybe gentle's not the right word." She snipped the cloth.

"Pinch?"

"What, Mom?"

"When I think of Sorrow, I think of a weeping willow tree. It's a very friendly tree, Pinch."

"I know it, Mom."

"And when I think of Charley, I think of a young pine, or maybe an oak. They stand up there looking at you, and maybe throw acorns or pinecones at you."

She worked at cutting out square pieces of cloth for her quilt for a long time. Then she looked at me.

"You are warm to Sorrow 'cause there is a sweetness about her. I am warm to your dad 'cause there is a strength about him. Maybe that's what the difference is, Pinch. When your dad's around I get a kind of glowing feeling. Things are said between us, even when no words are spoken. Been that way as long as I know him."

She held up the four pieces of cloth she had sewn into a square to see how they fit.

"No need to be jealous of the crane, Pinch. Sorrow is still your friend."

15

A Certain Trust

I WENT BACK to Sorrow's house. When I was sure nobody was looking, I headed through the woods for the crane pen. Sorrow was sitting on the cold, damp ground, staring at the crane, but the crane wasn't paying her one bit of attention.

I walked over and picked up the fish bucket and started toward the road and Blind River. I hadn't gone ten feet before I heard her running after me. Her hand touched my arm and I turned and gave her a little bit of a grin.

"A fellow can get pretty tired of playing with Charley," I told her.

Her eyes twinkled. She reached over and took hold of the wire handle so we could carry the empty bucket together.

In the few days I had been away, the bird had changed. The brown splotches were melting away. The crane was slowly turning pure white, except for the black mittens on the tip of its wings.

Other things had changed too. Sorrow wanted to

cuddle the bird but it wasn't about to let her do it. It wasn't interested in being anybody's friend.

I watched Sorrow trying to touch the crane. She turned quickly and saw me looking at her. She dug out her pencil and paper and wrote me a note.

"I think it's a girl crane," she wrote. "She is so beautiful."

The bird pranced around the yard, keeping its distance, staring at Sorrow every once in a while. She stood up and went in the pen and held out a handful of corn, standing perfectly still for the longest time. But the crane didn't seem interested at all. It was getting late. When the cold air got to me, I stood up.

"I'm going home, Sorrow."

She looked out at me and nodded, but kept standing there, hoping for the crane to come to her.

"Why does it stare at us like that?" I asked her. She clasped her hands, stared at me, and shrugged her shoulders.

When I got home I asked Mom the same question. She was darning one of Dad's socks.

"Suppose there was an animal and it was sick and you tried to take care of it and it wouldn't let you come close. All it would do is stare at you."

"What kind of animal are we talking about, Pinch?"

"Just any old animal."

"Well, son, if it was a dog, or a cow, or a mule, or even some pigs, that would be strange, 'cause there's a certain trust, say, between a man and a dog. But if it was a fox, or a rabbit, or maybe a skunk, well, that would be a pretty regular thing for it to do." She looked in my direction and there was a sparkle in her eye. "And porcupines, too, Pinch. I remember a time when a porcupine told you and your pig to keep your distance."

"But suppose it was a big bird?"

"I think big birds would feel about like porcupines do, son."

I told her how the crane would only stare at us.

"It doesn't really bother me much, but it does Sorrow. She would like to get up close and touch it."

"Pinch, you shared your secret with me. Now, I'll share one with you. Don't you tell Sorrow what I tell you, but it's probably the truth. That girl lost her paw only about a year ago. That's a terrible thing to happen to a child. Sorrow's got a wonderful maw, but one's not as good as two. Sorrow's looking for love anyplace she can get it. It's a perfectly normal thing for her to do." She put a few more stitches in the sock.

"But the bird just wants to keep its distance," I said.

"That's just the way things are, Pinch. That's the way love is. Love don't work the way Sorrow wants it to."

She put away her sewing needle and thread and stood up.

"Sorrow ought to find herself a puppy. Puppies know how to give love back," she said.

16

Toad-Watching

ALMOST ALL OF the brown feathers had dropped from the crane the day Mr. John Barrow came snooping in the woods. We heard him before we saw him and we rushed to head him off.

"What you children doing in these woods?"

"Looking for armadillos."

"Oh! Well, it'll be a miracle if you find one. What's that chicken wire doing out in these woods?" Bushes hid the crane from him.

"Got to have a place to keep the armadillo if we find it."

We had turned him around and were walking out of the woods, Sorrow on one side and me on the other.

"Pinch, don't you have no brains at all? That little critter was born to dig. He will be out the pen before you even turned your back on him." He flipped around and started walking back toward the pen. "Now let's go back there and I'll show you how to fix it right."

I held tight onto his arm. "We were just leaving 'cause of the snakes," I told him. That stopped him quick.

"What's that, Pinch?"

"Copperheads. Dozens of them."

"Maybe we jist better git out of here!" he yelled, whipping around.

By the time we got back to the road in front of Sorrow's house, he was back to his regular slow walk. When we got to the fence, he rested against a post.

"Seen any big white cranes around here, Pinch?"

I looked at him quick. He wasn't even looking in my direction. But Sorrow was, and there was fear on her face.

"Tell the truth," he said, "I ain't even interested in cranes at the moment. The Zoo Man's looking hard, but I got plenty other things to worry about. I still got a courting problem, and I ain't even started figuring out how I'm going to handle it." He was looking poorly, that was a fact. And he had pulled a piece of dry bread out of his pocket and he was chomping on it. It didn't help his talking any.

"Why, Pinch, you ever stop to think what would happen if that three-legged toad the teacher gave me up and died? I lay up half each night thinking about it. Why, the teacher'd never forgive me as long as I lived. Why, that might be the finish of it between her and me.

"And I'll tell you something else, if you promise not to tell a living soul," he said, finishing up on the bread and wiping the crumbs off his mouth.

We promised and leaned closer to hear.

"Well," he whispered, sneaking looks all around to

see if anybody was within hearing distance, "I don't even like that warty old toad!"

He stuck his hand in his pocket and pulled out another piece of stale bread and started chewing on it.

"It's a good thing I'm an honorable man, 'cause if I wasn't, I'd be sorely tempted to dispose of the toad and suffer for it, whatever the suffering might be. You got no idea the trouble it's been causing me." He sat down on the edge of the road to rest his skinny legs.

"I built him a box and I put a piece of blanket in it to make it soft. And I been giving him more flies than he will eat. You'd think he'd show a speck of gratitude. Well, he don't. He jist sits there and makes me worry. I lay in my bed nights worrying about his health. I hear a little noise and I think maybe he got out of his box and will squeeze through a hole somewhere and git outside where a snake can git at him." He turned to Sorrow.

"I tell you, Sorrow, there is no ending to the suffering a man will go through for a woman." He took to scratching alongside his head, on one side, then the other. His eyes stayed on Sorrow. Then he grinned a little bit.

"I'm still thinking about the big crane, child. If that bird *is* somewhere on Blind River, maybe I can git it if I tried. Cranes is good eating, Sorrow. Sweets told me you can bake 'em like a turkey." She flipped her back to him and started walking down the road. He turned to me. "Now, you stay here and talk to me, Pinch. I remember a man who used to take them big wing bones and boil 'em and clean off the meat and let the bones dry and then he would make whistles out of them wing-bones."

I started to walk off, but he shouted after me, "Wait a minute, Pinch. I ain't told you it all." I saw Sorrow stop up ahead, but she kept her distance.

"There's two things I got to do real soon or else I'm going to lose my health. I got to git me some sleep. I jist got to." He shook his head from side to side. "And I got to go and talk to that teacher. We got to come to some kind of understanding. Seems to me like a man ought to speak his will early in the game if he's going to have his say-so later on."

"When are you planning to go see the teacher?"

"Oh, maybe day after tomorrow, or sometime."

"Why don't you go today?" I pushed him.

"Oh, no, Pinch, I couldn't do that. I got to do some more thinking on it. But I tell you what. You could be a big help to me right now if you wanted to. You're a fine young fellow," he said, pouring it on like syrup. "I wonder if you'd be interested in taking care of the toad for me for a little while?"

"You mean you want to sell him to me?"

"Oh, no," he shook his head, "I can't do that, you know that, Pinch. You would jist take care of him."

Wasn't any gain in that for me.

I told him that the teacher had given the toad to him and she probably wouldn't agree to the idea of me having it.

Sorrow had been listening, and she ran back and

reached up and tugged at his shirt-sleeve, telling him she had something she wanted to say. She dug in her britches and pulled out pencil and paper.

"I'll keep the toad for tonight," she wrote.

First it was cranes! Now she was fixing to tend to a broken toad!

Mr. John Barrow popped up straight.

"Lordy, child, you are the sweetest thing there ever was. A night's sleep is all I need." They went off together to get the toad.

Sometimes Sorrow makes me feel ashamed. I could've kept the toad for a night or two so Mr. John Barrow could get some sleep. It wouldn't have hurt.

17

Last of Its Kind

I WAS LATE for school, so I rushed out the front door toward the road. Dad was in the yard, fixing the hinge on the front gate.

"You got a minute, Pinch?" He put the broken hinge on the ground. "Son, I saw what you and Sorrow got penned in the woods behind her house. Too bad about the busted wing. Maybe it will heal."

My head jerked up to look at him. It wasn't so much that he knew about the crane, 'cause I already told Mom. It was that he found the crane all by himself. Mr. John Barrow had almost done the same. The Zoo Man was probably right around the corner.

"I want you to know I got strong feelings about that bird. Hasn't been one like that around here in a long time. It may be the last one of its kind in the whole wide world. We don't know if it is or it isn't. For sure it don't belong in the Zoo Man's cage." He picked up the broken hinge and stuck it in his back pocket.

"Come on around back, Pinch. I want to talk to you for a minute. You'll make it to school on time, don't worry." He walked into the back yard, straight for the armadillo cage.

"Come over here, Pinch. I want to ask *you* a question for a change." I walked over and sat next to him. "What if I was to look at that armadillo and say to myself: 'Is this the last armadillo in the whole wide world?' The question would scare me, Pinch. Hunters and trappers don't ask themselves that kind of question. If they did it too often, they would stop what they were doing and maybe change to farming or storekeeping or something like that." He took my hand and squeezed it, not hurting, only holding.

"What would I do if that was the last armadillo in the whole wide world? Would I skin him and fry him? Would I stuff him and put him on a shelf where I could always be sure I knew what an armadillo looked like?

"Maybe I would spend all my time trying to find another armadillo so I could put the two of them together in a pen and tell them to produce a hundred more." He let my hand go. He was talking to me, but he was thinking about things he had thought about many times before.

"Pinch, you know that every time an armadillo has babies there are four of them? Every single time? That's a miracle."

He picked up a dead leaf off the ground and stared at it.

"I could turn that last armadillo loose and pray that

he would take care of himself. The problem is, suppose he didn't? Suppose the armadillo fell in a hole and died? That would be the end of armadillos."

He looked at me. It was the hardest look he ever gave me.

"Son, does a man decide for another man?"

"Maybe not," I told him.

"Sometimes we do, Pinch. Now I'll ask you another. Does a man decide for an armadillo or a big white crane?"

"I don't guess so."

"Men do, Pinch. Son, this is the hardest question I'm ever going to ask you, so think careful. When we don't know the right thing to do, do we cross our fingers and trust things will come out right? Or do we think hard on it and then make things happen the way we think they should happen?"

I didn't know what the answer was. The truth is that Sorrow wants to help the crane get well and free. The Zoo Man is all for putting the crane in a cage. For sure it will live a long time in a cage if it is taken care of.

But what is the right way? What does the bird want?

Dad walked over and opened the door to the armadillo cage. He backed off. The armadillo stuck its snout out the door and sampled the air. Dad walked back and put his arm on my shoulders. The two of us walked toward the front gate.

"Pinch, the chances are that sometimes the right thing to do is to make things happen your way. Other times, the right thing to do is let things be. Every time it stares you in the face, it's an important decision to make. Whenever you have to make it, I hope you do the right thing."

He gave me a little shove.

"Now it's time to go to school and get some learning," he said.

18

Copperhead

WHEN I GOT HOME from school that afternoon, Dad was working on the gate again. He had a brand new hinge in his hand and was about to nail it on when he saw me. He stopped working.

"Been waiting for you, Pinch. I want to get a good look at that big crane from close up." Mom was watching from the porch. She took off her apron and said she would like to go too. We headed down the road, talking while we walked.

"If anybody sees us, we are going to visit Mrs. Nix," I told them.

"We'll be careful, Pinch. Don't you worry," Dad said. We walked, listening to the noises of the woods.

"Listen to that mocking bird sing, Pinch," Mom said. "I guess I like birds 'cause I like music. Nothing prettier to wake up to in the morning than twittering birds. It's a dainty sound." She smiled at me. "I'm not talking about roosters, now, Pinch. A rooster'll squawk you up in the morning, all right. But a rooster barely makes it as a bird. More like a loud-mouthed lizard with wings and bad manners. You write down your ten favorite birds, nobody in his right mind will write down a rooster."

"You are right, Victoria," my dad said, smiling. "But if I was writing down my ten favorite dinners, chicken would be right at the top."

"Tonight's going to be fried chicken, Will Grimball, so you can quit your hinting about what I ought to fix."

We moved away from the road and into the woods before we got to Sorrow's house. She was at the chicken wire pen. She had the bucket of acorns and was trying to feed the crane. It had been eating from her hand, but moved off when we got there.

"Look at that big white bird!" Dad said. "It's bigger than you are, Pinch."

"Does it sing?" Mom asked. She went inside the pen and took a handful of acorns to help feed the crane. Sorrow nodded that it did. But the crane's bugling sound always sent a chill through me.

There were too many people around, and the crane walked slowly away to the other side of the pen. Mom switched her attention to the Rhode Island Red and her chicks that Sorrow had brought as company for the crane. Mom walked over toward them.

There was something on the ground!

"Here, little chick-chick." Mom knelt down on the ground near the chicks. She stuck her hand in her dress

pocket and pulled out a piece of white bread. She had
come prepared to feed a bird, crane or otherwise.

Something brown near the fence!

One chick came near and poked at the bread. It was
a pretty little yellow ball of fur. It started peep-peeping
and in a minute a half dozen little chicks were pecking
away only touching distance from Mom as she knelt on
the ground.

Something was slithering along the ground!

"Here, little chick-chick," Mom said. She reached
out and carefully lifted one up. She put it to her face
and nudged its beak with her nose. She was having the
best time of her life.

I looked at Sorrow, wanting to see her smile.

She was standing rigid, fists clenched, the bucket of
acorns laying on its side where she had dropped it. Her
eyes were on the ground, watching. Her mouth was
open to scream but no scream came. My eyes jerked to
where she was staring.

There was a copperhead slithering slowly across the
yard! It was after one of those baby chicks!

My mom's back was turned to the snake. She was
cooing to the chicks. Dad was watching her have her
fun. He smiled. He didn't see the snake.

Sorrow saw it! She couldn't yell. She couldn't even
whisper a warning. The yell was screeching from my
chest for Dad to help when the willow whistle sounded.

"Whhhhhooooo! Whhhhhooooo!"

Dad looked to Sorrow. The whistle was still in her mouth. She stabbed her arm toward the snake. The copperhead had crawled to the edge of Mom's skirt and stopped.

"Victoria," Dad said softly.

Her head came up slowly. There had been a warning in his voice and she had heard it in the single word.

"Don't move. Not an eyelid." He ran as he spoke. "There's a copperhead after the chicks and it's close enough to you to strike. Lord, Victoria, don't move."

The copperhead sat still, tongue darting out. Then it started to slide. The rustle of the snake on the cloth drove all the other sounds away. Mom heard. It was the loudest noise in the whole, wide world.

The crane watched the snake's every move. The crane's long black legs carried it slowly across the yard, head bobbing, yellow eyes staring.

"Hssssssssss!" It was the crane that hissed, not the snake.

It was over terribly fast. The crane lifted both its huge black-tipped wings and hopped in the air. The snake faced the crane and struck. The crane hopped again, dropping down, wings flapping, beak stabbing. The long, sharp beak pierced the head of the copperhead. Again and again. By the time Dad dashed through the rickety gate there was no life left in the snake.

Mom trembled. She stood up slowly. Dad was at her side. She held onto him for a minute. The little chicks kept pecking away at the bread. The crane moved to where Sorrow had thrown the acorns and pecked at one.

I walked Sorrow home. When we got to her house, there was a worried look on her face. She took out her pencil and paper and we talked.

"I saw the copperhead. I wanted to scream," she said. "If it had bit your maw, it would've been 'cause I didn't warn her in time."

When I got home, Mom had already put the fried chicken on the table. Dad was out back, fixing something.

"Wash up, Pinch, and help me finish setting the table."

I put out the plates and the knives and the forks. I mashed the warm potatoes and mixed in the butter and the cream. Mom carried over the plate of steaming fried chicken.

"Pinch, I was never so proud of Sorrow as I was this afternoon. If she hadn't warned us with that whistle when she did, no telling what would've happened."

After supper Dad and I sat on the front steps and talked about it.

"Son, a bird don't often go after a snake unless it can't do much else. I would've figured the crane to hop out of the way. Why did it attack? It didn't know your maw, and it sure wasn't worried about those little chicks. It's a strange bird, Pinch."

A brave one is what it is. It was protecting Sorrow is what it was doing.

19

A New Owner

IN THE MORNING I told Sorrow that now was the time to move the crane. The wing was healing, but not fast enough. Too many people were trying to find it.

There was worry on Sorrow's face. She took me by the arm and walked me through the dark woods to the pen. She brought me to the farther end. Right beside a big bushy oak the weeds had been trampled down. It was like somebody had made themselves a nesting place to sit and watch the crane.

"Who do you think it was?" But Sorrow didn't know.

We walked inside the pen to feed the crane. It was prettier by the day. All the creamy brown had gone away. It was pure white. A red cap was forming on its head. And the crane had changed in other ways, too.

The crane started for Sorrow the very minute we were inside. Sorrow pulled a little fish out of the bucket. The crane stared at it. Then its long beak reached up and plucked it out of her hand. She fed the crane another fish. She put her hand on its back and stroked it.

The crane tolerated that until the fish was disposed of. Then it walked over near the fence and turned around and stared at us.

But I had only seen the start of it. Sorrow motioned me to leave the yard with her. We went off a ways and stood, watching the crane. At first nothing happened. Then the bird lifted its black-tipped wings and flapped them softly up and down. The bad wing was almost as straight as the good one. Suddenly, too fast to tell, the crane started to run, wings pulling at air. It hopped from the ground, lifted high enough to clear the fence, and landed hard on the other side. It stuck its long neck up into the air and sounded its joy.

"Ker-loo!"

A friend was visiting a friend! I turned to Sorrow. "How long has it been doing that?"

She held up two fingers.

"Two days?"

She nodded. Then she motioned me to follow. We went back inside the chicken yard and stood perfectly still, and the same thing happened all over again. The crane flew back into the pen. Sorrow walked over slowly and touched the crane, very lightly. The crane turned and walked away from her.

"Why would it do that?" I asked. "Why would it fly back into the cage once it got out?"

She smiled. She took me by the hand. We sat on her back porch. She pulled out her pencil and paper.

"The crane says it could leave if it really wanted to," she wrote.

wagon. He looked at her one last time. Then he climbed up and gave his black mule a hit with a stick.

The next morning the crane wasn't in its pen. We looked for the Zoo Man all morning. When we finally asked Mr. John Barrow to help us, there was the crane, locked up in a little chicken pen with wire on top. The crane wouldn't be doing any more flying.

When Mr. John Barrow saw us coming, he held up an arm, saying stop!

"Stop right there. I don't want no strangers on my property."

"You better give Sorrow back her crane!"

"You two children, listen to this. Afore we do any talking about you gitting *my* crane back, you go over to that sweet potato patch and see what that bird done. My patch is ruined! That's for starters."

"It's Sorrow's crane," I yelled at him, but he yelled louder than me.

"Wait a minute, you ain't heard it all. That's a wild bird in that pen. I didn't steal it from you. You had it penned up and it got out. So it belongs to whoever has it, and I got it."

Sorrow stared at the crane. It was as if she didn't believe what she was seeing. She looked at me. She shook her head side to side. She was telling me it shouldn't be. Then she turned to Mr. John Barrow. It was like a trusted friend had failed her. She would be crying soon if something didn't happen pretty quick.

"Why you staring at me like that, Sorrow? You angry at me?" he asked.

"It wasn't chasing a smelly fish you got hid i.
pocket, was it?" But I was only spoofing.

That wing got stronger every day. By the end o.
week the crane made long, low circles before sett.
down near Sorrow.

One of those flights took the bird straight up into th.
blue. It wasn't down five minutes when we heard th.
Zoo Man's mule and wagon dashing down the road.

"I saw it! I know I saw it!" He jumped down off the
wagon right in front of Sorrow's house and dashed into
the back yard. But we were waiting for him.

"Where's that crane? It landed practically in your
living room. You got it hid someplace? I'll give you a
dollar." But Sorrow just looked at him, not saying yes
and not saying no.

"I want that bird! I'll give you five dollars." She acted
like she didn't know what he was talking about.

"All right, little girl, I'll tell you what I'll do." He
was smiling now. First time I ever saw him smile. "I'll
swap you even for my little red puppy."

That time she heard him. I remember the first time
Sorrow had gotten close to that puppy. She petted him
and she let him chew on her fingers, laughing silently
the way she does.

But the choice she was having to make now wasn't
any fun at all. The crane needed her. Maybe more than
she needed the puppy. She looked at him and shook
her head again. It was a sorrowful kind of shake.

The Zoo Man walked angrily back to his black

She spun away from him and ran back the way we had come. Sometimes running is better than crying. But she didn't run far, 'cause it wasn't too long before we heard her coming back. When she came to the edge of Mr. John Barrow's front yard, she stopped. Then she walked kind of normal toward where we were standing.

She carried the toad box in her hand. She handed it to him. She had kept it for him practically all winter long, but he didn't look pleased at all.

"I hoped you could keep it one more night, child. I been sleeping regular and I would *really* sleep good if you could keep it one more night."

Sorrow stood there, holding out the toad. Finally he took it.

"Sorrow, don't you be angry at me, now. That's jist a bird back there. You know the profit I can git from that bird? The Zoo Man says two dollars, but I might even do better if I hauled it to the city myself."

Sorrow stared at him through wet eyes. I glared at him too, letting him know what I thought of him. From over in the corner of the pen, the crane's yellow eyes were staring. None of us spoke a word.

20

Whooping Crane

DAD SAID IT looked like Mr. John Barrow was stretching the law a little bit this time, but our stealing the bird back from him wouldn't be right.

"Why don't we walk across the road and talk with Tony? Maybe the law can help out here."

Mr. Tony wasn't any too pleased to be asked to be the one to decide.

"You know," he said, "sometimes being deputy sheriff can be a painful thing. The job don't pay hardly nothing at all. We don't really need a law officer in Four Corners. Trouble is, since we got a deputy sheriff, people tend to find reasons to put him to work."

He looked at Sorrow. Then he shook his head, worrying about what he would do.

"Let's go see John," he said finally.

When we got there, Mr. John Barrow was trying to feed the crane some of the acorns, but the bird wouldn't eat. Sorrow took an acorn out of the bucket and stuck it through the wire and the bird plucked it right out of her hand. Mr. John Barrow didn't say a word.

"John, we got a legal problem here. People don't just pen up other people's birds. My gray cow is running around loose all the time, and you never once penned it up and said it was yours."

"Tony, this wild bird don't belong to nobody except who has it."

Mr. Tony turned to Sorrow. He put his hand on her shoulder.

"Child, this is your bird."

"Ah, now, Tony," Mr. John Barrow moaned. "You can't do that."

"But Sorrow, there's one more thing," Mr. Tony told her. "There's the damage to John's sweet potato patch."

"That's right, so I'm keeping the bird!"

"Sorrow, this is the way it has to be. You get your crane back, but John's got a right to be paid for the damages the crane done to his property. That is, if John is going to be mean enough to ask for damages." He turned to Mr. John Barrow. "What about it, John? You going to take money from this child?"

"You seen what that bird done? About a hundred dollars' worth of the best sweet potatoes you ever saw."

I heard the Zoo Man's wagon coming down the road. He stopped. His eyes searched for the crane. When he saw it, he gave a big jump in the seat like he wanted to dance. It was the closest I ever saw to him being happy. He jumped down off the wagon and came running toward us.

"You know what that bird is?" he said to anyone listening. He didn't even wait for an answer. "It's a whooping crane, that's what. Not more than a handful left in the whole wide world. The whole wide world! And you are looking right at one of them."

"Must be a pretty valuable bird," Mr. John Barrow said.

"Probably not, John. Ain't too many people who would want to buy one. Besides, I already gave you the two dollars I promised if you caught the bird. From here on, I'm going to handle things myself. I'm leaving tomorrow early and taking the crane with me. I ain't moving from in front of this gate till it's time to go." He went back to looking at the crane.

"John, I'm going to sleep right here on the ground. You got a blanket I could borrow?"

"The price for loaning a blanket is three dollars," Mr. John Barrow said.

"Well then, I'll use my own," the Zoo Man said. "Just didn't want to get it dirty." He stared at the crane and the crane stared back. It didn't want to be in the little pen. Its yellow eyes were telling him that.

"John," Mr. Tony said, "you sold this bird to Mr. Autin before you even had him?"

Mr. John Barrow started scratching the dirt with his shoe.

"Well, kind of."

"You sure you didn't just walk over and take Sorrow's bird out of her pen?"

"Tony, you know I ain't a thief. Jist look what that bird done to my garden. Wouldn't make no sense for me to take the bird and then mess up my own garden, would it?"

"I don't know, John. Maybe it would. I got to do some more thinking on this. Meanwhile, Mr. Autin, I would appreciate it if you would just leave the bird where it is. We will do some more talking first thing in the morning."

Dad put his big hand on my shoulder.

"Pinch, you and Sorrow probably got some ideas of your own on what to do about the crane. But we will let things be until tomorrow. You hear me?" I said I did.

Later in the morning we got to school and I told the teacher where we had been.

"It's a whooping crane," I told the class.

Sorrow dashed to the blackboard.

"Its name is Whooper!" she wrote, then turned and smiled at the class, and the kids laughed and stomped their feet.

We spent the rest of the morning worrying about our whooping crane.

In the afternoon the teacher decided that what the class really needed was to get outside and breathe some fresh, cold air.

"We'll take a field trip," she said.

She marched the whole class down the road to see the whooping crane. We made so much racket walking down the road that the Zoo Man was waiting out in front of Mr. John Barrow's house when we got there.

"I don't want a bunch of snotty-nosed kids stirring up my bird," he yelled.

"I just want these children to see Whooper. They may never have such an opportunity again."

"Well, they don't have one now," the Zoo Man said. " 'Less they got eagle eyes, they don't 'cause nobody's going to get closer than the road."

"Mr. Autin, if that really is a whooping crane, it certainly doesn't belong to you. It belongs to the world. Why, you didn't even catch it. Mr. John Barrow told me he was the one. Now you certainly don't want to deprive these children of seeing something they may never have the opportunity to see again." She wasn't exactly angry. She was just letting him know she felt strongly about the subject.

"Little lady, you got your problems, I got mine. Who you suppose pays the feed bill for all the animals I get? It's me, that's who. Where you think the money comes from to buy the food? From people who want to see the animals, that's who. Now, do they pay you money to teach these snively-nosed kids or don't they?" He was looking at me, but I didn't even have a head cold. "Well, I got to make my living too."

That would probably have ended it, except right at that moment Mrs. Pauline Nix came walking by, trailed by two of her little kids that were too young to go to school. When the Zoo Man saw her he whipped off his hat and stuck it under his arm. He nodded a deep nod.

"Good morning to you, Mrs. Nix. How is the family?"

Mrs. Nix nodded back to him and kept walking. But the Zoo Man probably figured if he started up a conversation with Mrs. Nix, the schoolteacher would be polite enough to move on and take all us kids with her.

"Something I got to talk to you about, Mrs. Nix," he said in a real serious voice.

She stopped and gave him a hard look.

"I just wondered if you ever saw a real, genuine whooping crane. You think your little kids might want to take a look? It's probably the only one for a hundred miles around."

She was listening. Sorrow had told her about the crane. The two little kids tugged at her to let them go and see the animals. She didn't say anything. Finally she started moving toward the back of the house where the chicken yard was. The kids ran on ahead, shouting for joy.

"Wait a minute, now," the Zoo Man yelled, and ran after them. "Don't you touch a thing. Don't you scare that bird!" He tried to catch them, but he couldn't. Mrs. Nix followed at her own careful pace. She was probably thinking it was a relief to have somebody else chasing after the little kids for a change.

We stood out in the road watching all of this. Then the schoolteacher smiled.

"Come with me, class," she said. She walked into the yard. We were more than halfway to the wire pen before the Zoo Man realized we were coming. But the schoolteacher had him where she wanted him. He wasn't about to yell and scream at us kids in front of Mrs. Nix. The schoolteacher knew it, and I knew it too.

Me and Sorrow and Charley showed every kid in the class all of the animals. We made up a pretty good story about how the turkey lost its eye, but most of the kids walked off before we finished telling it. They wanted to play with the red puppy.

Me and Charley kept asking the Zoo Man to open up the brand new snake box. He said keep away 'cause it was deadly poison. He said it was a walking snake. When it wanted to, it could stand up on its tail and walk almost as good as he could. And it could eat wood, so we better stand back, 'cause it might just decide to chew its way out of the box and slither along the ground, looking for kids it could sink its green fangs into.

It wasn't any fun listening to that kind of talk. Snakes don't have green fangs. But even if he was joshing, I wasn't interested in seeing that particular snake anymore.

The Zoo Man didn't say one thing more to us until Mrs. Nix took her two kids' hands and said good-bye to him. Then he walked over to the schoolteacher and said in a very soft voice that if we didn't get away from his animals in two minutes he planned on doing some serious yelling.

The whooping crane stood on one leg and watched us leave.

21

Escape Plan

AFTER SUPPER Sorrow and I sat on Mr. John Barrow's back steps and watched the crane. The Zoo Man had settled in near the pen. He was fixing his own supper on a little open fire. He didn't offer to share it with us.

While we sat there, the two Sweet boys dropped by to take a look at the crane. There was a new padlock on the gate to the pen, and Billy and Henry spent more time checking it out than they did the crane.

Sorrow wrote me a note and I strained to read it in the evening light.

"Everybody wants the crane. Even Billy and Henry Sweet. We got to get Whooper out of there, Pinch!" She wrote it in red, like she was shouting danger.

Her idea was to wait until it was dark and the Zoo Man was asleep. Then we would come back and cut a hole in the chicken wire.

"I don't think it's a good idea," I told her. "It's like stealing."

"You can't steal what belongs to you, Pinch."

The way Sorrow was thinking, there wasn't any use to bringing the crane back to her house. The fight would just start all over in the morning about who owned the bird. She had tamed the crane. Now it was used to being around people and easy to catch. The thing to do was to get it away from Four Corners. Its wing was almost as good as new. It was practically ready to take care of itself.

"We will bring it to the other side of Blind River and turn it loose," she wrote.

Blind River is about a mile wide, and nothing on the other side but swamp and snakes and alligators. It's not my favorite place, but nobody would go way over there looking for a bird with a hurt wing.

"Dad already told the Zoo Man the boats are full of rot. It wouldn't be safe for us. Mr. Tony will handle it. Mr. Tony already said the crane belonged to you."

"Won't you help me, Pinch?" She held the pencil so tight, I thought it was going to snap.

"Nothing will happen to it before morning."

"It could die. Cages kill things."

"I don't want to do it, Sorrow."

She stood up and dusted off the seat of her britches. I couldn't see what was on her face. She went over to the crane and said good night. She didn't nod to the Zoo Man. I waited for her to come back and talk some more, but she never did. She walked slowly to the road and headed for home.

I went home and climbed in bed, thinking about the

crane. I couldn't sleep. The bed was hard. It was too cold. Sorrow was out in the dark somewhere.

All for the crane! Ever since we'd found it, Sorrow hadn't cared about anything but making it well.

"Ker-loo!" the bird sings when it is happy.

I turned on my side and thought about Sorrow wanting to free the crane. How could she know how it feels to be in a cage?

If you can't talk, is that like living in a cage? Wouldn't she have told me?

Maybe she had. She wanted to sing when she was happy. She told me that. She wanted to yell and scream when she was mad. She wanted to be able to tell her feelings when she was sad. She told me all those things.

I closed my eyes. I could see Sorrow at the boat dock. There was a bright moon. She was laying on the ground, resting. But the ground was moving. It was wet. Little waves lapped against her face.

She was floating in the water.

Maybe she would drown!

I had to save her! I had to help her cut the chicken wire and paddle the oars. I dressed fast and warm. The house was dark. I slipped out the back door and ran into the cold night air.

22

Blind River

SORROW AND I each pulled an oar, and at first the rowing wasn't too hard. We had a piece of moon to light our way. It got harder to see as the shore got closer. The darkness seemed to close in.

There was water in the bottom of the boat by the time we nudged land. My feet were ice where the freezing water had soaked into my shoes. Whooper lay in a sack in the bow where it was still a little bit dry. I got out and pulled the boat a ways onto the land. Sorrow strained to pick up the sack. She stepped out. I could hear the water squishing from her shoes.

We opened the sack carefully and she soothed Whooper before letting her out. We knelt there on the cold ground. Slowly I began to hear the night noises. Slithering sounds. Teeth chomping sounds. Sounds that whispered "snake" and "alligator" in my cold ear.

Sorrow turned the bird loose. There weren't any good-byes. They were just two silent gray shapes in the darkness.

"We better bail the water out before we leave," I told

her. We each took off a wet shoe and used them to bail. The water froze my fingers. My feet were ice. There was no feeling left at all. I tried to find the leak, but the water was coming in from a place I couldn't see.

I pushed off with an oar. We turned the boat and headed back, rowing hard. Sorrow was breathing heavy. It had been a long night. She started coughing. It seemed like she'd never stop. The wind was out of her. Suddenly, she turned loose the oar and held her hands to her chest to fight the coughing.

"Grab it!" I yelled, but the oar slid out of the lock and into the dark water. The boat began to turn. A cloud covered the moon as I began backwatering to keep the bow pointed toward where I thought the boat tie-up was. The cloud stayed over the moon.

Sorrow's coughing racked her body and shook the boat.

"Sorrow, I got to row! Move to the back and sit still!"

She moved to face me. I lifted the big oak oar and put it into the other lock. It was wet and cold and made of stone. I held it tight. It would get us to shore. It would get us out of the cold. It would get us to a warm, flickering fireplace.

And then I felt the water lapping at my shoes.

"Can you bail! Sorrow, can you bail!" I nudged her with my foot.

She had been sitting still, eyes closed, numb to the cold around her. She stirred at my words. She coughed again. But when the coughing stopped, she began to bail the freezing water from the boat, stopping often, breathing heavy.

"We're going to make it! I know we are!" But I couldn't even see the shore. The clouds still blocked the moon. I didn't even know if we were heading in the right direction.

When the clouds cleared the moon I could see the boat tie-up far down the shore to the left. But there was sand beach straight ahead. I searched for the bottom with the oar and poled the boat until it nudged the shore.

"Sorrow?" I touched her. She opened her eyes. Her body quivered. "It's all right. You got to get home and out of those wet clothes." She gave me a weak smile.

"We got to run," I told her. I helped her out of the boat. Her legs shook and would barely hold her up. We stood still for a moment. Then we started down the moonlit road.

I had to get her to run. The running would be good for her if she could do it. She needed her blood to heat up. She needed the running and warm clothes and hot soup and a blazing wood fire to stand in front of and feel the heat baking into her.

We ran. It was some of the most important running we ever did.

23

Questions

"I GOT HER bedded down now, Pinch," Mrs. Nix told me, still rubbing sleep out of her eyes. She laid Sorrow's wet clothes on the back of the kitchen chair and moved it closer to the stove. "That girl's got better sense than to go boat riding in the middle of the winter." She was looking me over pretty sharp.

"Mrs. Nix, I got to get home and into some dry clothes."

"Well, there'll be time for questions later. Get on home. Sorrow's resting under a stack of wool blankets and the shivering has stopped. But I mothered six children and I know the signs. She's going to get sicker before she gets better."

I went home and straight to bed. Nobody was awake to ask questions.

We were eating breakfast when Mr. Tony Carmouche knocked on the door.

"Morning, all," he said. "You excuse me for calling so early, but I got to talk to Pinch."

"Sit down and drink some coffee," my dad told him.

He sat. When he had finished his coffee, he put his cup down and looked at Mom, then Dad.

"Victoria and Will, you excuse me for asking your boy questions." He turned to me. He was being very serious.

"Pinch, John Barrow called me over to his place first thing this morning. The Zoo Man was there. No way to describe them both but being angry. It was more like they were spitting fire. There's a big hole cut in the chicken wire pen, and the crane is gone. Anything you can tell me about it, Pinch?"

I shook my head.

"Did you cut the wire, Pinch?"

I shook my head.

"Did Sorrow do it?"

I shrugged my shoulders.

"Are you answering the question, Pinch?" my dad asked.

"I didn't see her do it."

"O.K., Pinch. I thank you for your help." Mr. Tony turned to Mom and Dad. "This ain't where I want to be. John ought to be doing his own chasing around, trying to find out what happened to that bird. But John says he is too tired. He says nights he don't sleep well. He didn't tell me why. Maybe a guilty conscience from penning up Sorrow's bird."

He stood up. "I'm going to walk over and talk to Sorrow. Then maybe I'll have a chat with Billy and Henry."

Sorrow was too sick to talk to Mr. Tony, and he didn't get any help from the Sweets. The Zoo Man rode out of town in his black wagon, yelling that he was coming back in a week and if Mr. John Barrow knew what was good for him, he'd better find that crane and get it back in his chicken yard. Or else!

24

Visitors

I VISITED Sorrow mornings and afternoons for almost a week. I helped her mom feed her broth. Sorrow mostly lay there flushed and wore out. The only time she would perk up a little bit was when we talked about the crane. I told her Mr. John Barrow was looking every place he could think of, but he wasn't finding anything.

"Sorrow, he says he thinks he saw a big white bird flying near the south end of Blind River. You think the crane could really fly that far?" The look on her face told me she hoped so. "You know, maybe that other big crane is still hanging around." She didn't have anything to say to that.

"You feeling all right?" She gave me a little smile.

I told Mom about Sorrow's cold hanging on so long and Mrs. Nix saying maybe it was going to get even worse.

"Don't worry, Pinch. Sorrow is a strong child. She'll be on her feet in a day or two. I'll pay her a visit as soon as she can have visitors." She looked at me. Then she put her attention to the dust rag she was using to wipe off the dining room table.

"We'll bring her some of my vegetable soup. She likes my vegetable soup even more than you do, Pinch."

That wasn't true. Hot soup, with potatoes and beans and tomatoes and hunks of beef and orange circles of fat swirling around in it, is the best eating ever. What I do is butter up a big piece of French bread and dunk it in the hot soup and take a big bite and chew. It's the best thing there is. It is almost as good as Mom's hand-turned vanilla ice cream.

Mrs. Nix finally decided that Sorrow was well enough to have some more visitors.

"You tell folks, Pinch. Maybe it will do her some good."

Mom brought the hot soup and carried it straight to Sorrow. She was sitting up in bed with her drawing things. She put them aside and smiled weakly at us as we came in.

"Now," said Mom, "no matter how sick you are, my soup's going to make you well." She put the pot down on the side table and gave Sorrow a big hug. Mrs. Nix went and got a bowl and a spoon. Mom sat down to have a talk with Sorrow while she ate the soup. Mom isn't a person to just give things. She likes to see them used.

"I'm going to tell you how to get well the fastest way possible." She smoothed out her skirt in her lap like it was an important thing to do. While she was doing it she looked quickly at me and there was a twinkle in her eye.

Sorrow took the spoon from her mother. It slipped from her fingers and dropped into her lap. She looked at her mother and gave a little shrug. Then she reached again for the spoon and started in on the soup, slowly spooning it to her mouth, like the spoon weighed a hundred pounds.

"I know your mom is taking good care of you, but maybe there's a few things she don't know. You know, before she married Jeremy, your mom was a city girl." Sorrow and Mom had played this game before. It always ended up in everybody laughing.

"I changed the recipe for this particular soup," Mom said. "Guess you didn't know it, but fried hearts of rattlesnakes is good for colds. So I put some of them in the soup. You can taste them in there, can't you?" Mom took to nodding, and Sorrow looked up from spooning the soup and nodded back. Both of them were being serious about it.

"And live snails and little baby frogs is good for colds, too," she said. "So I put some of them in." Sorrow didn't slow up the spooning of the soup. "Two snails and about a half dozen little baby frogs." Sorrow choked a little bit on the soup. "I took out the snail shells," Mom said, straight-faced. Sorrow finished off the last spoonful of soup and plopped the bowl down in her lap like she was saying she was the winner. Mom hadn't been able to make her laugh.

"Ground up the snail shells and threw them in Pinch's corn flakes this morning, and he never knew the difference," Mom went on.

Sorrow's laughter was a soundless thing that shook her whole body. It was a joy to see. Her eyes squinched and her white teeth showed and little dimples in her cheeks danced with her happiness.

It's a fact, I told Mom, that the corn flakes tasted stale and as hard as nails. But they weren't that hard.

There was a knock on the door. It was Mr. John Barrow, and he came into Sorrow's room slow and sorrowful, with his hat in his hand.

"I brung you this here flower," he said and stuck it out to Sorrow. It was a black-eyed susan. I had seen a pile of them growing in the ditch in front of Sorrow's house. Normally Mr. John Barrow is kind of loud, but this time he wasn't. He was being soft and gentle and a little bit hangdog. It was almost like he felt guilty and was trying to make up for it. He turned to Mrs. Nix.

"And I brung this here clean sock," he said.

Mrs. Nix looked at the black sock that dangled from his hand, but she didn't show any intention of touching it.

"Take it," he said. "It's a gift. It's pure wool, and it'll make Sorrow well." He poked it closer, but she backed off. "What you do is turn it inside out like I already done and wrap it around her throat tonight. Watch out that you put the foot part of the sock on the sore part of her neck. Tomorrow morning she'll bounce out of that bed like she always does." He poked it out. "Go on, take it. I washed it good my very own self. It even smells clean and soapy."

Mrs. Nix didn't want to make him feel bad, so she got a paper bag and told him to drop it in the bag and she promised she would do the right thing with his sock at the proper time. We heard another knock on the door, and she left the room.

"Another visitor," she said, coming back with Mr. Tony Carmouche in tow.

"Hello, everybody," he said, then went over and gave Sorrow a kiss on the brow. "You get out of this bed as soon as your maw will let you. Best medicine for you is sunshine."

"What about fresh cow's milk?" Mr. John Barrow asked.

"Can't do a bit of harm." He turned to Mrs. Nix. "You need milk, you let me know. I got plenty." Then he turned to Sorrow. "But this here's what's going to make the child well." He stuck his hand in the sack he was carrying and pulled out a little box.

"Pencils," he said. "Might be thirty different colors there. Three greens at least. Hope you draw a lot of pretty green pictures with them." He handed them to Sorrow. It was a gift to make a girl happy. "Got them from the city this morning," he said. "Special."

While Sorrow was checking over her colored pencils, he turned to Mrs. Nix. "I got some other things here too. You can use 'em if you want 'em." He dug in the sack.

"My missus sends over the jar of honey and the fresh lemons." He pulled them out. "I can vouch for them. Lemon juice is good for a cold, and honey makes it palatable." He handed them over and started digging again. When he finished, he pulled out a little sack on a string.

"A camphor bag," he said, holding it out for everybody to see. "Kind of smells bad, but I sell quite a few of them. You wear it around your neck and it's supposed to keep the chills away."

Mrs. Nix took it from him, but she wasn't too anxious about doing it. But Mom nodded her head.

"Something more than superstition involved here, Pauline. Hang it around her neck. It'll do some good. I seen it used once or twice. It smells so bad, it probably chases the germs away."

The one that had to do the smelling was Sorrow. When her mom tied it around her neck, her whole face puckered up. She pinched her nose with her fingers, but it didn't help much. Then there was a knocking on the door and the Zoo Man marched in, not waiting for anybody to open up for him, and we all forgot about the camphor bag.

"What's that awful smell?" he asked loudly.

"What smell?" Mom asked. "Don't smell a thing."

"Hello to you, Mrs. Grimball. Nice to see you."

"Mr. Autin, would you do me the favor of talking softly in this sick girl's room?"

"I will, ma'am," he said, but he didn't do it. I don't think the man knew how to talk softly.

He walked over and stuck his hand out to shake hands with Sorrow.

"Shame you are sick, child. I brought you something that ought to perk you up. You just stay right there." He turned around and went back outside. When he returned, he was cuddling something in his arms. First he looked over at Mrs. Nix, and when she nodded, he moved closer to Sorrow's bed.

"I always felt that sickness was partly in a person's head. You give them something to fiddle with and take care of and clean up after, and the sickness generally goes away."

It was the red puppy.

Sorrow looked from the man to the dog. There were tears in her eyes. She reached out for the pup and he gave it to her. First she cuddled the little pup in her arms and let him chew on her fingers. Then she looked up at the Zoo Man. It was a nice thing that he did. She looked at him long and hard. When he caught her looking at him, he kind of smiled.

"No, child, this ain't got nothing to do with the crane. This is a present from me to you. That's a genuine dog. Don't know for sure what kind, but he's genuine."

She petted the pup. The crane was safe from the Zoo Man for now, anyway. She had kind of tricked him, but there wasn't any reason to feel guilty. It wasn't *his* whooping crane. It wasn't *anybody's* whooping crane. The crane belonged to itself.

But the Zoo Man didn't give her a lot of time to think

nice thoughts about him. He turned back to Mrs. Nix and started his regular shouting.

"Why ain't this child in the hospital?" he yelled. "Why ain't a doctor here looking at her? You know how sick she really is? What's that smelly bag doing hanging around her neck?"

Mrs. Nix stared him down.

"That dog clean?" she asked him.

"Course, it's clean. Nearly drowned from the scrubbing I gave him. You think I'd bring a dirty dog in this house?"

"Sorrow thanks you for the dog. It's a nice present. I thank you too. You got any more business here, or is it time for you to leave?"

The Zoo Man was hoping for a little more hospitality. Her words set him back for a minute. He was used to having people pay attention to his yelling. But it had never bothered Mrs. Nix, and he didn't know how to deal with that.

"I'm not leaving," he said. "I just got here. I'm visiting. And I'm being nice as I know how."

"You spend an awful lot of time yelling for someone who is trying to be nice!"

He thought about it for a while. He looked around the room, staring at each one of us in turn. He spent a long time looking at Sorrow and the puppy.

"I can't help it," he said. "It's the way I am."

Mom looked at him. "You're basically a good man, Mr. Autin. Maybe you'll grow out of the yelling."

He looked across at her. He knew she was joshing at

him, and he didn't like being joshed in front of Mrs. Nix, but you could see he had decided to show he could hold onto himself.

"Thank you, Mrs. Grimball."

Mr. John Barrow had been watching all the goings on without saying a word. In his mind I knew he was going over every inch of ground around Four Corners, trying to figure the whereabouts of the crane.

Suddenly he stood up and said his good-byes all around.

"Where you going, Mr. John Barrow?" I asked him.

"I been thinking hard, Pinch. I jist thought of something I hadn't never thought of." There was a sly look on his face. Sorrow and I had seen it before.

25

The Decision

HE WAS RUSHING down the road, kicking up dust. I had to run to catch up with him. He heard me coming, turned and slowed down, pulling on his chin like he does sometimes when he is thinking hard.

"Mr. John Barrow, those boats are rotten and full of leaks!"

"What's that? I don't need no boat, Pinch. And you can't stop me, so no use trying."

"What are you going to do?"

"What I should've done all along." He pulled on his chin some more. "You know, Pinch, I been thinking. When somebody gits sick like Sorrow done, you tend to think about them harder than normal. Maybe they will die." He looked straight at me to make sure I was following what he said. "Don't you worry none, Pinch, 'cause Sorrow ain't going to die. She's jist got a little cold." He walked a ways further without saying anything. Then he turned to me. "Son, I been thinking some more about the schoolteacher, and about that no-count toad of hers, too. Suppose it was me that died,

Pinch? Suppose I never got a chance to say to her what I want to say?" He stopped walking and nodded his head ever so slowly. Then he started walking fast.

"Goodbye, Pinch. I finally decided what I'm going to do. Today's the day I'm going to tell the school-teacher what I want to tell her."

I never believed he'd go courting! I still didn't. It was some kind of trick.

I followed him home every step of the way. He changed into his paw's old suit, and I followed him to the schoolhouse. He went in the front door.

Nothing happened for about a year. I was sure he'd snuck out the back window when the front door flung open and Mr. John Barrow marched out with a big smile spread across his skinny face. His scrawny chest was stuck out front and his head was held up high. When he saw me he turned, walking toward me like a happy strawman, his paw's old coat flying every which way. Before he even got close, he started shouting.

"Pinch, I done it! It surely makes a man feel good, finishing something he sets out to do!"

He grabbed me by the shoulder and pulled me along. It was hard keeping up with him, but I had to know what happened inside the schoolhouse.

"Where you going?" I asked him.

"I'm going home, Pinch. I'm going to take off this fine suit and git me some rest. That's what a man needs after slipping out from under a mountain full of worries."

toad. I hope you got your fifteen cents with you, 'cause he's all yours now."

Well, that stopped me cold. When he finally looked back, he yelled some more for me to catch up, but I wasn't about to do it.

"Mr. John Barrow, I sure don't plan to *buy* the toad," I hollered to him. He turned around but he kept walking backwards up the road.

"All right, then, Pinch, if that's the way you feel, I'll sell the toad to Charley. He offered me a lot more money anyway. I don't want to do that, Pinch, 'cause I'd hate to have to suffer that miserable toad one more night. But you can't expect me to *give* him away. Why, nobody jist *gives* things away." He stopped and I walked up to him. "You can have him for a nickel, Pinch?"

"Mr. John Barrow, the teacher said you could *give* the toad to *me*. She didn't say you could *sell* it to Charley or anybody."

He was frowning hard, and he started to scratch his skinny head like he always does.

"Well, she might've said it, but she didn't mean it. When she said 'give' she really meant 'sell.' Now, that's jist good reasoning."

"Mr. John Barrow, it would upset her something terrible if I told her you were going to go against her true meaning and not *give* the toad to someone she said to *give* it to."

"You wouldn't do that, now would you, Pinch? Not

He kicked some stones out of his way and pulled me along with him while the words flowed out of his mouth like a pump handle was working his jaws.

"I tell you, son, I never knew I had the courage in me. I walked in the door and there she was, putting away books or something. She said: 'Why, Mr. John Barrow!' And I said: 'Yes, ma'am.' And she said: 'Good evening to you.' And I said the same. And then I waited for her to say something else, but she didn't. So I said: 'I don't think it's going to rain.' And she said: 'Oh, I'm glad of that.' We kept on talking like that for the longest time. Both of us was kind of fired up, I guess. I asked her if there was something I could do to help out and she said: 'No, thank you.' I was kind of hoping she would say something about Paw's suit, but she never did."

All of a sudden, Mr. John Barrow slammed to a halt right in the middle of the road and grabbed hold of my shoulder.

"Pinch, you got to hear every word of this, 'cause here's where it starts gitting good! Why, she spoke right out about it! She didn't hold back at all. She looked at me with those big blue eyes of hers and said: 'Mr. John Barrow, how is our friend, the toad?'

"Now, Pinch, I didn't expect her to bring the subject up right away. But I played the same kind of game she was playing, and I said: 'Why, I guess that toad's doing all right.' She said she was glad to hear it. I took that for another good sign. She was standing across the desk from me right then, Pinch, so I moved jist a little bit closer. And that's when I done it! My paw and maw would've been proud of me. And you too, Pinch."

He was a happy man and I was happy for him, but when the folks in town heard about it, there was bound to be some talk about whether or not the teacher is right in the head.

"Pinch, I told her that when I got through asking what I was going to ask, if she had any strong feelings, why she should jist go right ahead and git them off her chest. I told her I knew feelings was the strongest things there was. She said, yes, she did too. I told her that if the answer was 'No,' I would understand. But I was sure hoping this wouldn't be a 'No' answer. She was beginning to fidget, so I figured I better git right to the point. I braced myself and looked her square in the eye and asked her:

" 'Teacher, it's about the toad. Would you mind very much if I loaned him to Pinch for a few days so I can git some sleep?' "

26

The Toad

I KNEW IT all the time! I knew he didn't have the courage to speak his mind to the schoolteacher. He kept right on jawing.

"And, Pinch, you know what she said? She said, why, it was perfectly all right with her. And you know what else she said? She said, why, if that toad was causing me any bother, I could jist *give* him to you permanent, 'cause she didn't want me to be bothered over any old toad. Why, Pinch, she couldn't have been any nicer if she tried." He started walking again.

"Mr. John Barrow, I thought you went in there to tell the teacher you were sweet on her?"

"Oh, no, Pinch, I guess you was confused. It was a matter of clearing the ground between the two of us. You got to start at these things real slow. I forget sometimes that boys don't know some of the things us growed men know."

He moved ahead of me and I had to run and still I lost ground. He yelled back to me: "You keep up with me now, Pinch. You come on to my house and git your after all I done for you?" He slowed down. Then all of a sudden he stopped and turned on me. He was an angry man.

"I'll give you the toad on one condition," he snapped.

"I sure don't plan to agree to it until I hear what it is," I told him. You don't rub noses with Mr. John Barrow without learning something about bargaining.

"Pinch, if anybody asks you about this, you got to say you paid fifty cents for the toad. Will you do it, Pinch?"

I told him I could live with that. He took hold of my sleeve and tugged, pulling me down the road toward his house. So I let him. I made him give me the special-made box and the piece of blanket and a half dozen flies he had in a bottle. He tried to sell me some extra flies he had hid away somewhere. I told him I could catch my own flies, but he didn't seem to hear me. He sat up there in a hard-backed chair, eyes staring right at me. But he was sound asleep and snoring away.

I went home and put the toad and his box under my bed. Then I went and sat on the front porch steps and wondered how much sleep Mr. John Barrow would need before he decided to go crane hunting again.

27

The Hunt

IT TOOK ANOTHER whole week for Sorrow to get well enough just to step out of bed. Even then she coughed up a storm and wasn't too steady on her feet. Everybody in town took credit for her getting well so fast. Mom said it was her soup. Mr. John Barrow was sure it was his sock. But what he didn't know is that Mrs. Nix had used the sock to line the box she set up for the puppy to sleep in. Puppy stayed healthy, so maybe it worked. Mr. Tony Carmouche wasn't sure if it was the camphor bag or not. He put more stock in the honey and lemon. The Zoo Man had his money on the puppy.

"Good to see you up and around, child," the Zoo Man told her one crisp morning when we were on our way to school. "Glad to see the pup got you on your feet." He paused a moment. "You never did tell me how you came to get soaking wet in the first place." She didn't do it then, either.

Mr. John Barrow came plodding toward us. He'd been looking for the crane sunup to sunset and hadn't been able to find it.

"You'd of started looking sooner, you'd of found the bird by now," the Zoo Man yelled at him.

"You are looking at a man who needed his sleep," Mr. John Barrow said.

"John, I don't give a hoot about you being sleepy. You want to help me find the crane, you meet me by

the Blind River boat tie-up in an hour. I got to go col-
lect the Sweets. They are going to help."

The Zoo Man said he didn't mind Sorrow and me
following around while him and the Sweets and Mr.
John Barrow looked for the crane, but we would have
to stay way back. He didn't want to frighten the bird if
he spotted it. And he cautioned Sorrow to take it easy,
'cause she still needed her rest.

They put their heads together and decided that the
crane had to be on this side of Blind River, even if Mr.
John Barrow had already looked there pretty good.

Me and Charley and Sorrow got to the boat tie-up
first. A few minutes later, along came the men, but that
wasn't all. Trailing behind them was the Zoo Man's red
hound dog, sniffing at everything in sight. If the crane
had been on this side of the river, that dog might've
been the difference between us winning or them.

They split up, with the Sweets going one way down
the shore and the other two men and the dog going the
opposite way.

"You Sweets keep your eyes open, and no drinking
on the job. The bird can hide pretty good if it wants to.
We'll meet back here about noon and if we ain't found
the bird, we can decide what to do next."

We had to get to school, but at lunch we ran back to
the boat tie-up. They hadn't got back yet. Sorrow
started drawing pictures and me and Charley tried to
get in some fishing while we waited. The Sweet boys
were the first ones back.

"Looks like you boys are going to have to buy your fish at the store," Henry said.

"Looks like you boys are going to have to buy your whooping crane at the same store," Charley answered.

"Now, just hold onto your lip, Charley Riedlinger," Henry said. "We are tired and we are thirsty and we are hungry and we are in no mood to listen to smart-alec boys." They each found themselves a tree to sit down and lean against.

The hound dog was the next one to show up, still sniffing everything in sight. He even ran over and gave Billy Sweet a lick on the jaw. Billy fought him off and the hound moved over toward Henry, but Henry yelled, "Git!" and the hound turned around and ran back the way he'd come. The Zoo Man turned up about two minutes later with Mr. John Barrow trailing behind.

"Not one single sign of that bird!" he yelled. "Not a track in the mud! I didn't even find a dropping bigger than a sparrow's! Somebody's been trying to pull a fast one, but it ain't going to work."

Then he looked over at us.

"What you children doing here?" he shouted.

"Nothing."

"What's that mean. Nobody does nothing!"

"Just fishing."

"What you drawing, Sorrow?"

"Nothing," I told him.

"Pinch, you be quiet. I'm talking to her." He walked

over to take a look at the drawing, but Sorrow bent over and covered it with her body like she didn't want him to see it.

"Let me see what's on that paper, child." He was standing over her. I was pretty sure he wouldn't hurt her or anything, but it was scary, him standing there. It was hard to tell what Sorrow was thinking. At first she didn't do anything. Then she slowly uncovered the drawing and handed it up to him.

It was the whooping crane, flying away. Its great white wings were spread wide, black legs tucked behind, yellow eyes staring straight ahead. I looked at Sorrow. There was a spark of mischief in her eyes.

"It's gone and you'll never find it," I told him.

He looked at the drawing. It was a beautiful picture, and part of him was admiring the drawing. But the rest of him was still set on finding the bird. He handed the drawing back to Sorrow.

"Ain't likely that bird's wing healed so fast. You children ought to be trying to help me instead of hinder me. But your being here tells me something." There was anger in his voice.

He marched back toward the road with the hound following him. The Sweet boys just sat there. They didn't want to quit resting so soon, but the Zoo Man gave them such a hard look that they hopped up on their feet and trotted after him.

"Maybe it really did fly away!" I yelled after him, but he didn't even turn around. He is mad most of the time. Now he was downright angry.

He kicked some stones out of his way and pulled me along with him while the words flowed out of his mouth like a pump handle was working his jaws.

"I tell you, son, I never knew I had the courage in me. I walked in the door and there she was, putting away books or something. She said: 'Why, Mr. John Barrow!' And I said: 'Yes, ma'am.' And she said: 'Good evening to you.' And I said the same. And then I waited for her to say something else, but she didn't. So I said: 'I don't think it's going to rain.' And she said: 'Oh, I'm glad of that.' We kept on talking like that for the longest time. Both of us was kind of fired up, I guess. I asked her if there was something I could do to help out and she said: 'No, thank you.' I was kind of hoping she would say something about Paw's suit, but she never did."

All of a sudden, Mr. John Barrow slammed to a halt right in the middle of the road and grabbed hold of my shoulder.

"Pinch, you got to hear every word of this, 'cause here's where it starts gitting good! Why, she spoke right out about it! She didn't hold back at all. She looked at me with those big blue eyes of hers and said: 'Mr. John Barrow, how is our friend, the toad?'

"Now, Pinch, I didn't expect her to bring the subject up right away. But I played the same kind of game she was playing, and I said: 'Why, I guess that toad's doing all right.' She said she was glad to hear it. I took that for another good sign. She was standing across the desk from me right then, Pinch, so I moved jist a little bit closer. And that's when I done it! My paw and maw would've been proud of me. And you too, Pinch."

He was a happy man and I was happy for him, but when the folks in town heard about it, there was bound to be some talk about whether or not the teacher is right in the head.

"Pinch, I told her that when I got through asking what I was going to ask, if she had any strong feelings, why she should jist go right ahead and git them off her chest. I told her I knew feelings was the strongest things there was. She said, yes, she did too. I told her that if the answer was 'No,' I would understand. But I was sure hoping this wouldn't be a 'No' answer. She was beginning to fidget, so I figured I better git right to the point. I braced myself and looked her square in the eye and asked her:

" 'Teacher, it's about the toad. Would you mind very much if I loaned him to Pinch for a few days so I can git some sleep?' "

The Toad

I KNEW IT all the time! I knew he didn't have the courage to speak his mind to the schoolteacher. He kept right on jawing.

"And, Pinch, you know what she said? She said, why, it was perfectly all right with her. And you know what else she said? She said, why, if that toad was causing me any bother, I could jist *give* him to you permanent, 'cause she didn't want me to be bothered over any old toad. Why, Pinch, she couldn't have been any nicer if she tried." He started walking again.

"Mr. John Barrow, I thought you went in there to tell the teacher you were sweet on her?"

"Oh, no, Pinch, I guess you was confused. It was a matter of clearing the ground between the two of us. You got to start at these things real slow. I forget sometimes that boys don't know some of the things us growed men know."

He moved ahead of me and I had to run and still I lost ground. He yelled back to me: "You keep up with me now, Pinch. You come on to my house and git your toad. I hope you got your fifteen cents with you, 'cause he's all yours now."

Well, that stopped me cold. When he finally looked back, he yelled some more for me to catch up, but I wasn't about to do it.

"Mr. John Barrow, I sure don't plan to *buy* the toad," I hollered to him. He turned around but he kept walking backwards up the road.

"All right, then, Pinch, if that's the way you feel, I'll sell the toad to Charley. He offered me a lot more money anyway. I don't want to do that, Pinch, 'cause I'd hate to have to suffer that miserable toad one more night. But you can't expect me to *give* him away. Why, nobody jist *gives* things away." He stopped and I walked up to him. "You can have him for a nickel, Pinch?"

"Mr. John Barrow, the teacher said you could *give* the toad to *me*. She didn't say you could *sell* it to Charley or anybody."

He was frowning hard, and he started to scratch his skinny head like he always does.

"Well, she might've said it, but she didn't mean it. When she said 'give' she really meant 'sell.' Now, that's jist good reasoning."

"Mr. John Barrow, it would upset her something terrible if I told her you were going to go against her true meaning and not *give* the toad to someone she said to *give* it to."

"You wouldn't do that, now would you, Pinch? Not

All of us trooped back toward Mr. John Barrow's place. My dad and Mr. Tony were talking in front of the store.

"What's going on?" my dad asked.

"We been bird hunting," the Zoo Man said.

"All you grown men chasing after one crane?" Mr. Tony asked.

I took Sorrow's drawing from her and handed it to Mr. Tony. "Look at Sorrow's picture. The bird is gone." I smiled at him and he winked at me.

"Ain't that interesting," he said. "Everybody in Four Corners has his own plan for that crane. Then it flies off all by itself. Didn't need anybody's help to do it. Mighty interesting that the bird had a plan all its own."

The Zoo Man stood there, red-faced and sizzling.

"You people are having your fun at my expense. You think I don't know it? You think I don't know where that crane is at this very minute?" He turned to Mr. John Barrow and took him by the shoulder.

"John, we've been looking hard on this side of the river. No place for the bird to be but on the other side. I know it now. I should've known it all along. Somehow that little girl brought it over, and now she's standing there with her angel face like she don't know what I'm talking about."

Only Sorrow's eyes moved. She stared at him. He stared back. The staring lasted for the longest time. But it was him who finally broke away.

"John, I need your help. I don't trust myself with no more help than Billy and Henry." The two Sweets were standing not ten feet away, listening to every word, and not pleased at all at what they were hearing. "And, John, I ain't too partial to swamps, anyway. Would you go over there and find the crane for me?"

Mr. John Barrow stared at him. You could see that he was interested, even if he *was* poking a finger in his ear and trying to look like he had other things he'd rather do.

"What you offering?"

"Maybe ten dollars. I might go that high."

"Twenty dollars."

"What!"

"And your big mule. I never owned a mule as pretty as that one."

The Zoo Man clenched his fist like he was about to show he could hit better than the mule could kick. Then he kind of dropped his shoulders like he was surrendering. He gave Mr. John Barrow a sickly smile and stuck out his hand.

"All right, John. You got a deal. I want that bird worse than I want that mule. Even if it'll hurt my business until I get me another one."

"Why, Mr. Autin, I plan on giving you my fine mule as part of the bargain," Mr. John Barrow said. "It eats too much for the work it does, anyway."

He didn't tell him that it is swaybacked and toothless and full of flies.

"When you going to start looking, John?"

"I got oyster shells to haul this afternoon. I can cross the river first thing in the morning."

I looked at the Sweets. Their mind was on that twenty dollars that they weren't going to share in. There was a mean look on their faces.

I looked at Sorrow. She was looking at me. We had until morning. It wasn't much time.

28

The Sweet Boys

SORROW AND I decided we would bring the crane
back to this side of the river as soon as school let out.
The afternoon took a year. There were so many things
I wanted to talk to Sorrow about, but we didn't get a
chance until recess.

"Maybe we need to bring the net."

But she didn't think so.

"I'm going to bring a sack. It'll cover up the white-
ness of the bird," I told her.

There were too many kids around to do any real
talking. About the time the teacher rang the bell, Mr.
John Barrow passed by with his wagon load of oyster
shells. He had the new mule in harness, so he must've
been pretty sure of himself. We went back inside for
more waiting. I wrote Sorrow a note and passed it
to her.

"I think we ought to bring the net."

When I looked up, the teacher was standing over me,
arms folded across her chest. She stuck her hand out to
Sorrow, asking for the note. She read it. She looked
from one of us to the other.

"After school we will talk about this." She walked back to the front of the room.

The teacher said we should take out our history books, but I wasn't interested in history. *Now* was the important time! Sorrow pulled out her book, but she didn't pay any attention to it. She wrote furiously. When she finished she sat there, looking at the school-teacher. I waited for her to pass me a note, but she didn't pay me one bit of mind. She was waiting for something. Then the teacher asked the class a question and Sorrow's hand popped up before anybody.

"All right, Sorrow, come on up to the blackboard and write the answer."

She jumped up and dashed to the front of the room. She didn't look at the blackboard one time. She handed the teacher the paper with all that writing she had done. The teacher stared hard at Sorrow for a minute. She began reading the note. First she would read a little, then she would look at Sorrow. When she finished, she folded the paper in half and gave it back to Sorrow.

"Class," she told the rest of us, "we are going home early today."

She didn't have to say it twice. There was a bolt for the door and two seconds later only me and Sorrow and the teacher were in the room.

Charley stuck his head in the doorway: "Pinch, you coming?"

"Got to stay after school," I called back.

There wasn't any talking after that. The three of us headed straight for the boat tie-up.

But not soon enough!

Mr. John Barrow's wagon and mule sat out in the field. He had decided not to deliver his oyster shells after all. He wasn't anywhere to be seen.

He'd gone after the crane!

We ran to the rise near the water and there he was, already pulling oars for shore. The crane lay in the stern of his boat, wrapped in a fishing seine. He didn't see us until he started dragging the boat out of the water.

"Oh!" he said.

"Mr. John Barrow!" the schoolteacher shouted. I never saw her so mad. She twisted her hands around each other and looked at the crane laying still and not moving a feather.

"I am truly disappointed in you!"

Mr. John Barrow had been trying to keep a stern look on his face. But the anger of the schoolteacher softened his look. He kept his eyes on her for a minute. Then he lowered his eyes to the ground. There was no way he could defend himself. The evidence was a pile of white feathers and staring yellow eyes right there in the boat.

"Don't say nothing," he said. "Won't do a bit of good. I got a bargain with the Zoo Man and I'm going to deliver the bird to him right this minute."

None of us said a word. The teacher shook her head side to side, ever so slowly. Sorrow just looked at him.

"Don't do that to me, Sorrow," he said and turned away from her stare to look at the new mule.

One by one we climbed in the wagon and sat, without even asking him. The silence was like a funeral procession. Sorrow moved back in the wagon where she could comfort the crane. The crane just lay there, watching. There wasn't a thing it could do.

"Ain't nobody going to talk to me?" Mr. John Barrow asked.

Nobody did. We reached Burnt Corn Bayou and followed it for a while, everybody thinking their own thoughts until we came around the turn near where the Sweets live. There they were, standing in the middle of the road, waving their arms and acting silly. They were drunk is what they were. Henry stood on a big old log that floated a couple of feet out into the bayou. The water was so cold, there was a dead coon laying on the bank, froze stiff. Henry was trying his best to spin the log, but it was too big for him to budge. Billy stood right in the middle of the road. He grabbed our brand new sorry mule and stopped us.

"Howdy." He turned to Henry. "Look what we got here! A schoolteacher, a smart-alec boy, the best bird catcher in town, and a little girl that don't like to talk." He walked around the side of the wagon. "What you got in the back of the wagon, Mr. John Barrow? Looks like a very valuable bird. Don't know how you caught it, 'cause *we* are the best bird catchers in Four Corners. Maybe we ought to just steal it like you done and sell it to some zoo ourselves."

Mr. John Barrow told Billy he should let the mule go and get out of the way, but Billy wouldn't do it.

"Me and Henry are just looking for a little fun," he said. Then, quick as a flash Billy ran around back of the wagon and scooped Sorrow in his arms and ran to the very edge of the bayou. The teacher screamed and Mr. John Barrow yelled for him to stop. Even the mule got excited about it. Billy whirled Sorrow up in the air and chunked her out over the ice-cold water right into Henry's arms. He teetered back and forth on the log and for a second it looked like they both might be gonners. Then he caught his balance and stood up, holding her like a baby and smiling his silly smile at us and breathing clouds of whiskey breath in her face.

I jumped down out of the wagon and headed straight for Henry, but Billy yelled for me to stay put 'cause if I kept messing around Henry might get a cramp in the arm or something and drop Sorrow. And she was sure to catch a death of cold if she fell in that icy water.

"Mr. John Barrow, unless you want Henry to get a cramp, you unhitch your mule and tie him to that bush over there."

Mr. John Barrow gave him a look that could have killed a sober man, but he went over and did it.

"Now, you hitch yourself to that wagon like you was a mule."

Mr. John Barrow stood there, tall and skinny, just staring at him. Then he snorted like an impatient horse.

"Billy Sweet, you boys going too far. You better git while you can." He stood there and glared at them until Henry yelled he was getting a cramp. Then he did like they told him to.

When Mr. John Barrow was hitched up, Billy told
the teacher to pick up the reins, and Billy jumped in the
back of the wagon with the crane. He told Mr. John
Barrow he wanted him to pull the wagon in a large
circle around a big sycamore tree that was sitting out in
the pasture.

"I figure that to be about twelve feet times twelve
feet," Billy said to the schoolteacher.

Mr. John Barrow leaned into the reins, but the heavy
wagon didn't budge. He turned around and dug his
heels into the dirt and the wagon began to move. But he
found himself staring right into the face of the teacher,
and that was more mortification than he could take. He
faced front again and put every bit of strength he had
into it, and finally the wagon started to roll. He inched
his way toward the sycamore tree, puffing every step of
the way, making it around and heading back. His
breath came out in big clouds. As cold as it was, his face
was bathed with sweat. He blinked it out of his eyes.

The teacher was having her problems too, sitting up
straight in the wagon, tears running down her face from
the shame of it. She took hold of my hand but didn't
say a word.

Billy stood up in the back of the wagon looking like
he had just won a turkey shoot. He swigged on his
bottle and laughed and tried to do a dance, but the
wagon wouldn't let him. Finally, he finished off his
whiskey and yelled: "Whoopee!" He threw the empty
bottle on the hard ground and jumped off the wagon
right about where it all started.

Mr. John Barrow stopped pulling and stood still for a minute, puffing to get his strength back. Then he un-hitched himself and waited to see what kind of foolish-ness would happen next.

Henry tossed Sorrow over the icy water to Billy one last time and Billy set her on her feet. She rushed toward the wagon and I rushed toward her. When Mr. John Barrow saw that she was free, he reached under the wagon seat and pulled out his double barreled twelve-gauge shotgun and leveled off on them. The Sweet boys would have been dead in their tracks for sure, but the teacher reached down from the wagon seat and put her hand on his shoulder.

"They're drunk, John. Let them be."

That shotgun was pointed right at their middle, but the teacher's words ran a shudder through him and you could see him take hold of himself. He lowered the shotgun and stood there with it shaking in his hands.

Billy and Henry looked at that big gun and looked at Mr. John Barrow. When they saw that nothing was going to happen, Billy grinned and then Henry did too.

"We are pretty good bird hunters, Mr. John Barrow. You ain't the only one." They turned their backs and trotted down the road. Then Billy turned his head around and yelled.

"Maybe we'll just show you how good we are!"

29

Harness and Willow Switch

WE DROPPED Sorrow off at her house. Her eyes begged Mr. John Barrow to leave the crane with her, but he quickly looked away.

"Night, Sorrow."

When we got to the teacher's house, she asked us in. She said it was terrible, the things the Sweets had done, but the best thing to do was forget it.

"John, I want to talk to you about that crane."

"Won't do one speck of good. I already been paid the twenty dollars and the mule. A man's got to live up to his word."

She talked to him for about a half hour, telling him this was one bird that was going to die if it got put in a cage, and if he *did* sell the bird, he better not come around the schoolhouse ever again with his sickly smile and his dirty overalls. But all the talking didn't do one speck of good.

She opened the front door for us and stood there, scowling. When we got to the wagon, the crane was gone.

"The Sweets got the crane!" Mr. John Barrow yelled.

"Good!" yelled the schoolteacher and slammed the door.

On the way home he didn't say a word, till all of a sudden a shudder ran through his body. It was something more than the cold.

"I ain't never held a gun on a man before in my whole life," he said. For the rest of the ride to my house he was quiet. I climbed down from the wagon.

"Good-bye, Pinch."

"What are you going to do?"

"I got some thinking to do, Pinch." He gave the reins a little flip and moved away.

About an hour later there was a knock on the front door. Mr. John Barrow stood there with his shotgun in his hand, broke open, and he was putting shells in it. He was being mighty serious about it. I asked him what was going on and he said he had a plan. I should go back inside and drink some hot coffee-milk and dress warm, 'cause we were going to ride in the wagon again. So I did it. I told Mom I'd be with Mr. John Barrow and I'd be home before bedtime.

We stopped first at the teacher's house, then at Sorrow's. Our next stop was in front of Billy Sweet's house. Mr. John Barrow banged on the door, and when it popped open he pushed his way inside. A little while later Billy came out with Mr. John Barrow following, his shotgun trained on Billy's backside.

Everybody got in the wagon and we went further

down the road to where Henry's house was and col-
lected him, with Mrs. Sweet moaning along behind him.
We walked out in a cow pasture across the road from
Henry's house.

"You two boys are cold sober now, ain't you?" Mr.
John Barrow asked them, and they said they were, a
little bit. "So where's the crane?" But they just looked
back at him like they didn't even know what a crane
was.

"All right," he told them, "that's the way it's going
to be, you two strip down to your long johns!"

The ladies cried "Ohhhh!" but he turned on them
and gave them a hard look and they shut up quick.

For a minute it looked like Billy and Henry didn't
understand what he was telling them to do. Then they
started taking off their clothes. You never did see two
scrawnier-looking men than those Sweet boys standing
there in their long johns. They were big men, but
they had skinny legs like some big men do. Even fat
Henry. While they were skinning off clothes, Mr. John
Barrow sent me and Sorrow out to stick up tree branches
in the ground. The branches made a big square, with
us standing in the middle. When we finished, he sent
us to the wagon to unhitch the mule and bring him the
harness, and we did it. He threw the harness to Billy
and told him to harness up Henry, 'cause it was time for
the fun to start and Billy was going to do the driving.
Both of them just stood there looking like they didn't
believe him, so he pulled one trigger on that shotgun

and a load of buckshot tore into the dead willow branches over their heads. They jumped a foot with the noise and got the harnessing work done.

"And here's a willow switch to make your mule do your bidding," Mr. John Barrow said, handing it to Billy. Billy took hold of the switch, but Mr. John Barrow didn't let go his end. Instead, he jerked Billy so close that the shotgun rammed his belly button.

"Billy Sweet, I want that crane!" he hissed.

Billy stood there, kind of dumb-looking, holding onto the reins with one hand and the switch with the other. His mind wasn't on cranes. It was on driving mules. He must've been thinking that if it had to be this way, it sure was lucky that he got elected Driver instead of Mule. It was his nature to get the most fun out of things. So he backed away, and even before Mr. John Barrow got around to yelling at him again, Billy grinned and he gave the willow switch a snap and cracked it right across Henry's rear end. Billy yelled, "Haw!" and Henry yelled, "Ieeeee!" right at the very same second, and off they went, running around the square at a pretty good clip.

I never saw a man so pleased with himself as that Billy Sweet. He smacked his mule with his whip and gave him free rein, and then when he got him going good, he reined him in, yelling loud at him every minute. Old Henry spent more time turning his head around, looking at his driver with meaner eyes than mules generally do. And it was a real hard look he was giving him, I tell you. I could almost hear him thinking: "Mr. John Barrow's gonna make you be mule next, and then you gonna get it."

They made about half a dozen passes around the field, with Billy having a real good time and Henry not enjoying it much at all. Each time around, Mr. John Barrow hissed at Billy: "Where's the crane?" but Billy would only look over at us to see if we were having as good a time as he was.

Mr. John Barrow stood tall, shotgun ready, not a sign of anything on his face. But not me. I couldn't help doing some smiling. Sorrow shook softly with laughter. The teacher tried not to show it, but she was smiling some too. And Mrs. Henry Sweet was doing best of all. She started laughing so hard, she pulled her shawl up over her head so nobody could see.

Billy finally figured a grown man running around a cow pasture in his underwear just had to be making a fool out of himself. The two of them kept on going at a slow trot, 'cause Mr. John Barrow still had his shotgun trained on them, but you could see Billy wasn't having fun any more, and for all his hoping for a chance at being driver, neither was Henry.

They had about got back to where they first started when Billy yelled: "Mr. John Barrow, the crane's in Henry's kitchen, keeping warm. Can we stop?"

"You mean it's in the oven?" Mr. John Barrow yelled angrily.

"No, just keeping warm," Billy yelled back.

"That's enough!" he told the two of them.

"Now it's my turn," Henry said.

"No it ain't," said Mr. John Barrow. "We got something more important to do." He gave them another of his hard looks and pulled his shotgun up high. It was quiet. He broke the gun open and kicked the good and spent shells out of the barrel. He clicked the gun shut, bent over slowly, and laid it on the ground, watching them two every minute.

"Now, if you boys think you got anything coming back to you, this is the time to try and git it." He squared his scrawny shoulders up and both hands curled into fists like cypress knots. He stood waiting.

It got quiet again. The ladies breathed heavy. There weren't any other noises. Mr. John Barrow stood up there like he could do it all day. But nothing happened.

Finally Henry Sweet said: "Mr. John Barrow, we sorry for hitching you to the wagon. We sorry we took the bird. We was angry at the Zoo Man. Maybe we had something coming. Let's leave it be. I'm froze stiff and I got to get something inside me to warm up."

That ended it. Mr. John Barrow got the crane out of the warm kitchen and put it gently into the back of the cold wagon. Then the rest of us piled in.

Nobody said a word on the way to drop off Sorrow and the schoolteacher. Not a sound came from the back of the wagon, but we knew the crane was there. When the ladies had been dropped off, I turned to Mr. John Barrow.

"It's Sorrow's crane! You want it. The Sweets want it. The Zoo Man wants it. But it's Sorrow's crane. You know it's Sorrow's crane. And worst of all, you almost filled those two men with buckshot because of it."

He didn't answer. He just looked at me. He was thinking about it. I felt certain that for the first time he was at least thinking about it.

"I got to earn money to put bread on my dinner table, Pinch. You and Sorrow are making it hard for me to do it."

He stopped the wagon in front of my house and I climbed off. He kind of nodded, but he didn't say good-bye.

I sat on the front steps awhile before going in. The wind was still there. It was as cold as it ever gets. The cold was making me feel small.

I never felt like a loser before this one time. It's a feeling that makes you want to hurt yourself and everyone around you. It makes you mean. I stood up and bumped into the front porch chair.

"Get out of my way, chair!"

I marched inside the warm house. Mom was sitting in the front room, sorting socks.

"What you been doing out in that cold, Pinch?"

"Nothing!"

"Been playing with Charley and Sorrow?"

"No!"

"Well, go to bed, Pinch, and sleep off whatever's bothering you."

30

My Dream

IN MY DREAM I knocked on Sorrow's door in late afternoon. When we got to the water, we could see the big white bird feeding down the bank.

Whooper was still free! Sorrow took hold of my shirt sleeve and twisted it tight. Her grip was so strong the blood stopped flowing in my arm.

I woke up and untwisted from the sheet. I put my head on the warm pillow and floated back into the dream.

The crane heard us and her head whipped up and those beady eyes stared us down.

Sorrow and I watched the crane watching us. Then the crane's eyes returned to the water, searching.

"Ker-loo! Ker-loo!"

The sweet bugle sound came from the sky. Mr. John Barrow had been right. The other crane was still around. It circled way up above.

"Ker-loo!"

It was calling to Whooper. It was warning her to fly from strangers who were really friends. But it was more than a warning. It was saying that it was time to leave.

Whooper looked up from the water, her head cocked over to one side as if she was listening for the first time to the call coming down from the sky.

"Whooper!"

Was it a thought or a sound? It came from right beside me and it tinkled like a bell in my ear.

A yellow eye fixed on Sorrow for a single moment.

Slowly, the way it happens in dreams, the big white bird stretched her black mittened wings out full. She flapped them against her side in a lazy fashion. She began a queenly walk through the shallow water, wings spread wide, neck stretched forward. The walk became a run. The wings ever so slowly stroked the air. She lifted and began a spiral upward, out over the river.

"Whooper!"

In my dreams Sorrow Nix sang to the white crane soaring into a cold blue sky. We watched the sky forever. The white crane slowly became a black dot. Then the black dot was gone and so was my dream.

31

Mr. John Barrow

MOM HAD A HAND on my shoulder and was shaking me gently.

"Wake up now, Pinch. Boys that go to bed late still have to get up early. Besides, you got a visitor. John Barrow is out front, and he says he's got to talk to you."

Coming around to say he's sorry after it's too late and waking me up early to do it!

He was sitting in the kitchen, drinking a cup of hot coffee.

"Hello, Pinch. Can we talk a minute?" He looked from me to Mom. She caught the look and she asked us if we would please excuse her, 'cause she had to go make the beds.

"Pinch, how is the toad doing?"

"What!"

"You ought to expect I'd be interested in the toad, son. You think back, you will remember it was me that first caught the toad."

Well, if there was ever a time I didn't want to talk about the toad, this was it. I turned my back on him and went to my room and got that toad. I set it out on the front porch, came back inside, and held the door wide open for him. If he wanted his toad, he would have to go outside to get him. When he did, I planned on slamming the door hard enough to shake it off its hinges.

"You don't need to hold the door open, Pinch. Gitting cold in here, and I ain't even ready to leave yet. Look a here, I still got half a cup of coffee." He tipped the cup to show me. "Besides, Pinch, the toad ain't why I came here." He took a sip of his coffee. "I came about the crane."

"What about the crane? You get rich from selling it?" I didn't budge from the door. I wanted it plain that he wasn't one bit welcome in my kitchen.

"I wasn't never meant to be rich, Pinch. Maybe a little bit contented now and then, but that's about all." He finished off his coffee and put the cup down. He looked me straight in the eye.

"Pinch, you ever feel that Sorrow talks to you?"

It was an odd question, but I had thought about it too. "Maybe."

"I don't mean with words, Pinch."

"I don't either."

"Son, could you close the door and sit here with me for a minute? I think you'll want to hear what I got to say."

I closed the door on the toad. Whatever was bothering Mr. John Barrow concerned Sorrow, and I wanted to hear about it.

"You remember when you and Sorrow came to my house that time after the crane was eating my sweet potatoes and I locked it up in my chicken yard?" He had probably stolen the crane, not found it, but I just nodded and let him tell it his way. "You remember what Sorrow did?"

"She went home and got your toad and gave it back to you."

"That too, Pinch, but even before that."

I didn't remember her doing anything but looking sad.

"She talked to me, Pinch. She did it with her big, brown eyes. All she did was look at me, but she was telling me she thought I done wrong." He looked down at his skinny hands, then looked up at me. "And, Pinch, you remember when she was sick in bed and we all paid her a visit and I brought her a pretty flower and a wool sock to make her well? She did it again that time. She talked to me with those big eyes of hers. She didn't want me out hunting for the crane while she was sick in bed." He leaned forward and put his elbows on the table, moving his skinny head side to side.

"She did the same thing to me yesterday, Pinch. She saw the crane in the wagon and her eyes told me her heart was breaking. She said it better than if she'd used a bucket full of words."

I waited a long while for him to say something more.

"That's all, Pinch. That's all I wanted to tell you." He stood up and carried his cup and saucer over to the sink.

"Except maybe one thing." He walked slowly to the kitchen door and opened it.

"Last night I turned that pesky bird loose near the boat tie-up. It flies pretty good now, Pinch. Ain't likely somebody's going to catch it again."

I looked at him. Would he fool around about something like this? But the happy grin on his face told me all I needed to know. I rushed to the door and to Sorrow!

"Pinch!" Mr. John Barrow yelled after me. "Can I really have the toad?"

"Mr. John Barrow, you can have a kiss from Sorrow and the toad from me!"

I ran into the cold morning air. Sorrow's crane was free! She didn't know it, and she was waiting to be told.

It's fun running in the cold. It whips at you. You close your eyes to narrow slits and you try to pull in air through your nose, but that never lasts. Soon your mouth is wide open and you are breathing deep and the cold air makes it feel like you have icicles in your chest.

Now I can tell Sorrow what it feels like to sing. It's when your chin is sticking up proud and you don't just want to talk or yell. You want a sweet tone to the things you say. And it's got to be loud. It's got to be loud 'cause you want lots of people to hear you sing. You want them to be happy with you.

I saw her in the distance, standing by the gate, schoolbooks in hand. My lungs pounded, but I ran faster still. I would be the one to tell her.